THE ASYLUM NOVELLAS

The Scarlets
The Bone Artists
The Warden

Also by Madeleine Roux

Asylum

Sanctum

Catacomb

THE
ASYLUM
NOVELLAS

The Scarlets
The Bone Artists
The Warden

MADELEINE ROUX

HARPER

An Imprint of HarperCollinsPublishers

For Mom, the strongest and best woman I know

A huge thanks to Andrew Harwell, Olivia Russo, and the amazing team at HarperCollins, who have helped grow this series year after year. Thanks as always to my incredible agent, Kate McKean, for working her many miracles. To my family and friends, thank you for putting up with my moods during deadline time; I couldn't survive the stress without you.

The Asylum Novellas: The Scarlets, The Bone Artists, and The Warden

Copyright © 2014, 2015, 2016 by HarperCollins Publishers

www.epicreads.com

ISBN 978-0-06-242446-4 (pbk.)

Typography by Faceout Studio

15 16 17 18 19   CG/RRDH   10 9 8 7 6 5 4 3 2 1

❖

The Scarlets and *The Bone Artists* were originally published as ebooks in 2014 and 2015.

First paperback edition, 2016

CONTENTS

THE
SCARLETS

Why be a man when you can be a success?

—BERTOLT BRECHT

There are always two deaths,
the real one and the one people know about.

—JEAN RHYS, *WIDE SARGASSO SEA*

PROLOGUE

*T*he things we want are only thus because we cannot have them. I myself desire a legacy that reaches beyond my own small life, perhaps even into immortality. When I achieve this—if, not when—it will surely cease to be the core of my longing. I crave and dread to know what I will want then. It will be bigger, yes, and accordingly it will consume me that much more.

—Excerpt from Warden Crawford's journal, spring 1953

*W*hen Cal woke up, the classroom was empty. No professor. No students. His cheek stuck to the desk a little as he jerked his head up. His mouth tasted sour and the world spun, everything skewed and fuzzy.

"He's in here."

That was his professor's voice. Professor Reyes. God, she was horrible. Cal couldn't stand her. That stupid gap in her teeth. The way she rolled her eyes when she posed a question and no hands went up. *Maybe you should ask better questions, lady.*

His head pounded, that sour taste in his mouth making his stomach turn. He put his head back down on the desk. It wasn't exactly comfortable, but it was better than keeping his eyes open and feeling the light pierce straight through to the back of his skull.

"This is the third time, Roger," Professor Reyes was saying. "Three times. It's unacceptable."

"I understand, Carie. Thanks for coming to me with this."

"Of course." Cal could just imagine her rolling those beady eyes of hers. "But next time . . ."

"Oh, I wouldn't worry." Roger—his dear old dad—managed a wry laugh. "There won't be a next time."

The door shut slowly but with a hard snap at the end, as if to

say she was leaving them alone but wasn't happy about it. Cal wasn't happy about it either. A new feeling knotted up in his gut, almost sharp enough to make him sick. But that might have been from the half case of Yuengling he'd had last night. The one that had made him pass out in class in the first place.

"Does this mean I can go back to Greenport?" Cal lifted his head again, this time smudging a tiny puddle of drool across the desk. "Please tell me I can go back to Greenport."

"I thought you hated Greenport. Couldn't wait to leave." Roger—it was always Roger, never Dad or Pop—hoisted up the girth over his belt before settling down on a desk facing Cal. The chair-and-desk-in-one squeaked in protest from the burden.

"Yeah, well, Greenport does suck. But this place sucks even worse."

Staring at his father was like looking into a magical mirror that showed Cal's future if he didn't lay off the cheap beer and Commons pizza. There was just the sparest tuft of reddish-brown hair on Roger's head, a few desperate wisps that he combed and gelled into an apology for his freckled bald spot. He had those freckles on his cheeks, too, darkening through his perpetual suntan. He had been handsome once, a fact his mother pointed out constantly until it wasn't so much affectionate as just really, really sad.

Your father was so handsome, Cal. Such a handsome young man.

Cal frowned, shifting his eyes to the floor. His mother could be so deluded. She still insisted on saying that crap even after the divorce, like maybe wishing could take her back in time. Frankly, Cal thought she was lucky to be rid of him.

"*Drunk*, Cal. Drunk in class? Three times?" Roger shook his head, making his drooping cheeks go all walrus-y and loose. "Thank God Caroline came to me. You're getting a reputation, son—a reputation I can't smooth over and pretty up for much longer."

"You poor thing."

"Sit up."

And Cal did. Sometimes, occasionally, he obeyed that singular tone of voice Roger had. It was the same voice Cal used to hear before getting taken over his father's knee as a kid.

"You know, some people would call this a cry for help."

Cal shrugged and worked a kink out of his neck. "Some people are idiots."

"You are not going back to Greenport." Roger crossed his arms over his chest, firming up his jowls into a sneer. "You are not going anywhere. You're going to stay here and get a tutor. You're going to sober up and stop this . . . this . . . these tantrums." He adjusted his tie and looked away, to one of the high, streaked windows. "I thought the gay thing was bad enough, but your behavior has only deteriorated since you started at this school."

"Gee, Roger, thanks." *The gay thing.* That sharp sickness in his stomach calmed. Roger was just trying to rile him up, get a reaction, and he wouldn't let that happen. Couldn't let that happen. "Did you like take a seminar on being a total dickhead, or does it just come naturally?"

He expected the anger, but he didn't see the slap coming. It hit and hit hard, and Cal felt his teeth slice open the inside of his cheek.

His father had been handsome once. His father had been an athlete once. His father had probably been human once, too.

Bastard.

"You will get a tutor," Roger repeated, wringing out his hand. "And you will sober up."

"And if I don't?"

His father stood and shimmied his belt again, staring down at Cal with cool, empty eyes. "I don't like making contingencies, Cal. Tutor. Sober. We won't be having this conversation a second time."

CHAPTER

2

*T*he words on the page blurred. Something behind his right eye felt like it was broken, like part of his eyeball had snapped off, leaving behind a blinding throb that wouldn't quit. He drummed his fingers on the desk, trying to disguise the tremor in his hand.

Less than four hours after his argument with Roger, here he was doing the tutor thing. The sober thing? Well, there was only so much a guy could tackle at once.

There were words in front of him on the desk and words ringing in his ears, but try as he might, Cal couldn't make heads or tails of their meaning or how they could possibly be relevant to him and his raging hangover, which hadn't gotten better even after all the aspirin he'd taken.

"Do you have any beer?"

Blinking, swallowing a yawn, his tutor stared back at him. She was cute, sort of, in the way only a quiet book nerd could be cute. She had tawny skin and shapeless, curly dark hair. Her teal eyes were the most conventionally attractive thing about her.

Those teal eyes were still staring at him. Right. *Fallon.* That was her name.

"You know drinking more won't really cure your hangover,

right?" Fallon asked, scratching at her cheek with the eraser on her pencil.

"I don't know and I don't care." Cal stretched, then thought better of it. Hunching over the desk seemed to be the only position that didn't rile his headache. "I just know that I want a beer right now, an ice-cold one, and that I want to know the bare minimum to write this paper on *Wide Sargasso Seat.*"

"*Sea.*"

"Whatever. This book is basically fan fiction for another, more famous book. Why are we even tested on this garbage?"

"Definitely don't put that in the paper," Fallon muttered, rolling her eyes. But she stood and shuffled over to the mini-fridge next to her bed and crouched, rummaging until she came up with a can of Bud Light. Maybe she wasn't such a nerd after all. "Here."

She put the can down harder than she had to on the desk, punctuating that one huffy word.

Cal managed a weak chuckle and cracked open the tab top. "On a diet?"

"Remind me to charge extra for this tutoring session. Sorry, charge your *dad.*" Not one for the jokes, then. That figured. Roger would've made sure whatever tutor he picked was totally humorless.

Just like Roger.

"What's he like anyway?" Fallon asked, so softly and casually that Cal wasn't sure he'd heard her correctly.

"Who?"

"Your dad. I've seen him a few times on campus, but I was surprised when he called me." Fallon was watching him intently.

Too intently for his liking. "I'm not an English major, and I've definitely never taken psych. Seems like there are better tutors for you on campus."

"Maybe you're the cheapest," Cal suggested.

"Right, like that's a big concern for your family." Rolling her eyes, she watched him fiddle with the icy beer can and seemed to interpret his silence as disagreement. "I thought you guys were loaded. And he's the dean. I hear he's got everyone in this place in his pocket—faculty, staff. . . ."

"Who told you that?" Cal asked, slumping down into his chair with a nonchalance he didn't feel. He took a sip of his beer to cover up the sudden flush in his cheeks.

Fallon turned to look out the window, the light coming in making her eyes even paler and more exotic. "Nobody *told* me," she said. "I just crack a campus newspaper once in a while. He's in like every other article, doing charity stuff, fund-raisers. Isn't he helping some local politician's big run?"

"What are you, president of my dad's fan club?" Cal sipped the beer, but it didn't have the numbing effect he was hoping for. "You need a new hobby, my friend."

Fallon closed her book and leaned on it, flicking her pale eyes between Cal and the can of beer. "How the hell did you end up here?"

About as quickly as he had lost interest in the assignment, he had also lost interest in the beer, and leaned back in the chair, fiddling with the chunky class ring on his left hand. "Here as in here?" he asked, pointing to his own chair. "Or here as in the college?"

"Take your pick."

"Stanford didn't want me. Princeton passed, too," he said.

"I can't imagine why," he thought he heard her mumble. More clearly, she said, "Daddy's money and influence didn't fix all that for you? I mean, you could be top dog on this campus, and it doesn't really seem like you are."

Ouch. Cal caught her eye, staring until she looked guiltily away. What was up with this chick?

"Well, to answer your question, I'm stuck here—at this college and in this chair—because dear old Dad's the dean, as you seem so happy to remind me," Cal replied with a withering sneer. "He only uses his money and influence to help himself, but because of him, I'm held to a higher standard."

"Are you kidding? I heard what happened in Professor Reyes's class. Anyone else would've been on academic probation or kicked out for good. I'd say mandatory tutoring is pretty damn lenient," Fallon said, and then in an undertone, "Pretty damn lucky."

What was he supposed to say to that? No? That he hadn't been silver-spoon-fed since before he could remember? He pushed away from the desk and stood, wandering to the dorm room window that overlooked the quad. Fallon had managed to snag a single in Jeffreys, which, for a second-year, was about as likely as getting hit by a comet and lightning in the same day. Cal moved the cheap Ikea curtain out of his way, squinting through the painful flood of sunlight to see the students milling around between classes.

Devon Kurtwilder and his buddies were having an impromptu lacrosse match on the grass outside Cal's dorm, Brookline. The whole thing could've been torn straight out of an Abercrombie

& Fitch catalog, chiseled abs and criminally tousled hair included.

If only he could get Devon as his tutor instead . . .

Cal also saw his friends Micah and Lara sitting under a tree not far from the lacrosse game. One of Devon's buddies passed a ball sharply to his teammate and it flew wide, nearly smacking Lara in her glossy dark head. Micah was instantly on his feet, all but beating on his chest Tarzan-style at the jocks. For a second, Cal thought the screaming match was going to escalate into a full-on fight. But then he saw his father striding up the concrete path that bisected the quad. Roger dodged onto the grass and came between Micah and the lacrosse players, saying something to Micah and waving around a manila file folder. Even after the players backed off and resumed their game, Roger kept waving the folder and barking at Cal's friends. Whatever he was shouting about, it made Lara gather her things and leave in a hurry.

Cal hoped this didn't mean anything serious for Micah—he didn't need to be getting in trouble. His roommate had had a rough life before college, but he worked really hard to be an upstanding student now. In fact, Micah had become the sort of model citizen at NHC that Cal had never managed to be. It had just taken a little help from Roger and a meeting with the admissions office to sweep Micah's record under the mat and get him into the school in the first place. According to Micah, anyway. It seemed like a fantasy to Cal. He didn't know that Roger.

If it was true, it was probably the nicest thing his father had ever done for anyone.

Cal left the window behind with a snort. A lot more than a pane of glass separated him from Micah and his father. "*Et tu,* Micah?" he said aloud.

"Can we get back to the novel, please?" Fallon asked in a huff, turning in her chair. She pulled her curls into a messy bun, the hair tie snapping so loudly it made him wince. "Or do I get to be your therapist, too?"

"My best friends here are dating," Cal said, as if that explained everything. He still insisted on making that distinction. His best friends *here*. He wasn't sure why. It wasn't like his friends from Greenport even thought about him anymore. They were all busy planning their bright futures as senators and governors, at Yale, Harvard. . . . "Not that it'll last. Lara will figure out what a boring goody-goody Micah really is, and that'll be the end of it. She says she finally wants a nice guy, but I know what a load of crap that is."

"Goody-goody?" Fallon laughed, a little bitterly, and glanced up from her book. "I heard that kid has a rap sheet."

"Oh my God, for *stealing*. In *high school*. It's not like he killed somebody!" Though honestly, Cal himself had found Micah's past intriguing when he met him last year. How often did you come across an overachieving, down-home charmer with a record?

"I always liked Lara," Fallon said softly, and with maybe a hint of disappointment. "She was in my first-year seminar. Brought a funny bear thermos to class every day."

"Yeah, she goes everywhere with that thing." Fallon seemed to know an awful lot about his friends, even though Cal had never seen her hanging around them before. Then again, NHC was a

tiny campus. He could probably name half of his year by name.

Cal ran his fingers across the spines of the textbooks and novels lining Fallon's crowded bookshelf. A few comic books were sticking out at the end. He chuckled and pulled one of them down. "Dudes in purple spandex, eh? Good choice."

"You can borrow it if you want," Fallon replied, finally shutting her book in resignation. "Although your dad would probably skin me if he knew we were reading comic books right now. You're supposed to be studying, Cal."

"*The Phantom*," Cal read aloud with a smirk, ignoring her. "The ghost who walks! Ooh, spooky! The purple getup kind of kills it, though, don't you think?"

"Seriously, take it. You'd probably like it. It's about a spoiled kid from a spoiled family who takes up his birthright to fight crime in the jungle. Maybe it'll work like magic and teach you something about what the rest of us peasants like to call *responsibility*."

"Oh, I know all about responsibility. My dad has been trying to make me be more responsible my entire life. Too bad for him he doesn't have any real power over me." Cal flipped through a few of the pages of *The Phantom*. "Anyway, I'm not sure I should be taking cues from a man in purple tights."

"I said you would like it, not that it was realistic." Fallon joined him at the bookshelf. She wore ill-fitting jeans and a simple gray tee with some kind of wolf-head design on it. Her chain-mail bracelet looked like it had come straight from a cheesy Renaissance festival. She seemed like the kind of girl who would really go to those things. "But you're right, you have better things to worry about."

"No, it's cool. I think I will take it," Cal said.

Fallon shrugged, but he caught a thin smile behind the show of indifference. "So what else do you have to do to convince your dad you're back on the straight and narrow?"

"Well, starting tomorrow, I have to sort junk in Brookline's basement," Cal replied with a groan, the thought temporarily squashing his upswing in mood. "Maybe I can convince Professor Reyes my delicate constitution can't abide the dust," he said, grabbing his book bag. "Anyway, thanks for the comic."

"No problem. And Cal?"

He paused on his way to the door, half turning his head to face her.

"I, um, I can do a thing or two with computers. If your dad doesn't let up, I could try and get into his email. Maybe there's something in there you could hold over *his* head for a change."

Cal chuckled, but it tapered off quickly when he realized she wasn't kidding. What she was proposing wasn't a bad idea, but he hadn't quite reached that level of desperation. "Thanks. I'll keep that in mind. But I can't pay you as much as my dad can. I can't pay you at all, really."

"Please. I'll be honest with you—your dad seems like kind of a dick," Fallon said, going to sit at her desk. She picked up a little USB stick and began fiddling with it. "And believe it or not, I know what it's like to have parents on your case. I could do this as a favor. It doesn't make us best friends or anything."

"Of course not."

Cal paused at the door, tucking the comic book into his bag with a quick wink. "Thanks for the offer. It'll give me something to think about after I finish this essay on Rhys's postcolonial

and postmodern response to *Jane Eyre*."

Before the door closed entirely, he got to enjoy a glimpse of her bewildered expression.

"What? I have ears. Some things *do* get through."

Fallon smiled and shoved a pen behind her ear. "Could've fooled me."

CHAPTER

3

Brookline basement. 7:00 sharp. Prof Reyes will let you in.

*C*al scowled at his phone and the irritating text message glowing up at him. This was not new information. Roger had emailed him instructions that morning. Did he really think it was necessary to police his every breath?

Cal started typing, *Stop worrying about me so much, you can't afford to lose any more hair*, then changed his mind and tossed his phone onto the bed. He and Micah shared a double in Brookline, which was almost awful enough to make him pledge a frat, if only to get a better room. He and Micah had ended up here after deciding to be roommates at the last second the previous year, but the irony was, Micah was hardly ever in the room now, since he and Lara had become inseparable. This was how it always was; things between Micah and Lara would be good for a few weeks and Micah would disappear. Then she would break up with him for a few days, or he would break up with her, and he would brood at his desk listening to weepy country songs until it drove Cal out of the room, to literally anywhere else.

Cal stared at Micah's empty, made bed. *You two are poisonous for each other. Hurry up and figure that out already.*

The privacy was nice, he supposed, turning back to his

computer and the open document on the screen. He had managed his name and "TITLE TBD"; then, a very long subtitle he planned to turn into a paper any moment now: "The descent into madness and cultural promises left unfulfilled—the true cause of Antoinette's deteriorated mental health in Rhys's *Wide Sargasso Sea*."

It wasn't bad, really, but that was *all* he had. One dynamite subtitle was not going to keep him from flunking out. Cal swore and saved the document, then let his black mood propel him like a missile to the shared mini-fridge. It was stocked with beer, as always, but crouching there and perusing the shiny cans didn't give him the jolt of anticipation it usually did. He knew if he drank right then, it would just be to secretly flip the bird at his father.

Instead, he slammed the door shut and went to crack open his window. Maybe air would help get the scholarly juices flowing.

The old Brookline windows hadn't been replaced since the sixties, when the building used to be an actual insane asylum. The school constantly closed and reopened the dorm, promising renovations that never seemed to materialize. The place felt like a tomb. The window shrieked as Cal forced it open, and a gush of moist air poured in. The lacrosse team was out on the quad again today—or had never left—their laughter drifting up to him like distant music.

"Hey! Kurtwilder! Over here, man, I'm open! Pass!"

Cal heard the words as if from a dream. He felt like he was only half-present—like he was watching the world below from somewhere that wasn't the world at all, and the scene before him was visible but not tangible. He imagined saying those words aloud, to Micah, maybe, or to Lara, and hearing how stupid they sounded. His friends would probably run to one of the college counselors, who would then tell him he was depressed. *Here, take this medication.*

Maybe that would help, he reasoned, leaning closer to the open window. He wondered if pills would make that invisible barrier between him and the world thinner or thicker. He didn't know which option scared him more.

As he stood there, he could all but hear the cursor on his screen blinking. Waiting. Ticking down the seconds he was wasting thinking about nothing. He could just drop out. That would be one way of handling all of this. Maybe he should call his mother, get her take on things. She had the kindness Roger didn't. But she wasn't exactly the best role model, either, since some of that kindness came from her nightly pills and vodka cocktail.

Cal glanced at his watch. Six thirty.

Half an hour. He could buckle down and be scholarly for half an hour, surely. He crossed from the window to his bed, where the book for his essay lay facedown and open, little Post-it flags indicating passages Fallon had highlighted for him. He flopped down onto the bed and grabbed the book, rolling onto his back and propping one knee on the other.

"'There are always two deaths,'" he read, "'the real one and the one people know about.'"

He was finally getting into the book when his phone buzzed right next to his head, making him start and drop the book on his face. Sputtering, he elbowed the novel out of the way and snatched up his mobile.

7 sharp, Cal. I mean it.

"Jesus, Roger, I get it."

It's like he can sense me procrastinating from afar. Saddest superhero power ever.

Groaning, Cal pocketed the phone and hunted down his book bag and shoes, a ratty old pair of Top-Siders his first boyfriend had given him in high school. Well, technically Cal had *stolen* the shoes, lovingly, and then Jules just hadn't had the heart to ask for them back. Cal would wear the damn things until they had holes and then find someone to repair them.

Brookline's halls were empty. It wasn't a popular evening hangout spot. Most kids he knew went to the library or the gym after dinner, sometimes to rehearsals or study groups. Even in broad daylight and at peak hours of activity, the dorm never felt cheerful. Crowded, maybe, but not lively.

That figured. There were all kinds of creepy-ass rumors about what had gone on in the bad old days of Brookline, when it was still an asylum and not just another historic fixture on a campus choked with historic fixtures. As far as he knew, it was mostly campfire crap, stories that got told around Halloween to spook the first-years and visiting prospies. He couldn't imagine what would actually be down in the closed-off basement. Certainly by now all of the important antiques and files had been secured and put away somewhere?

Cal whistled as he skipped down the stairs, determined not to spend the night in a dark mood. This was supposed to be punishment, but he would endure it like a champ. Hell, if he tried hard enough, he might even enjoy it. Maybe he could dig up a cool story or two for Lara to use in an art project. A lot of her work was about uncovering forgotten history.

He reached the main level and then continued downward, taking the turnoff toward the shadowy entranceway he had never given a second glance. Voices reached him from the alcove, and he passed a glass display case with some faded newspaper clippings, then took a sharp right, stopping short before he tumbled into someone's back.

"Ah. Our fifth is here." Professor Reyes poked her head around the human barrier directly in front of him.

Then Human Barrier turned, and Cal froze, squishing his toes nervously in his Top-Siders. It was Devon. Magical Lacrosse God Devon Kurtwilder, still sweaty from his game on the quad.

"Well, that's everyone, then," Professor Reyes continued. She was dressed in all black and half-wrapped in a glittery, beaded black shawl. About a dozen gaudy necklaces hung from her neck. "Let's head down, and I'll explain the rules as we go."

"The rules?" Cal repeated. He didn't recognize the other two students, but they looked older, maybe juniors or seniors, both girls. His dad had been on about how this was a "lucky group of students," handpicked by the professor to rummage around in the basement, cataloging whatever old stuff was down there. An Exploratory Committee, he'd called it, which sounded way too official and smart for Cal to be involved in any real capacity. So now he was a tagalong. Great.

Devon ignored him, snapping a piece of gum and turning back toward the professor. His shirt wafted cut grass smell and sweat.

Professor Reyes reached into one of the many crocheted

pockets on her tunic and fished out a giant key ring that wouldn't have looked out of place at Hogwarts. She swept them all with her dark, beady eyes and nodded solemnly. "There are rules to going down here, Cal. Rules to the basement. Rules to Brookline. There's more than just dust and memory down there; there are instruments, rusted but dangerous. So we have rules, and if you follow the rules, this will all go smooth as glass."

CHAPTER

4

*C*al hated the basement.

"How often do you guys come down here?" he whispered. It seemed important to whisper, as if the shadows lurking beyond the scope of the professor's flashlight could spread and come to life.

"It's a delicate process, beginning to catalog and sort the contents of Brookline," Professor Reyes explained from up ahead. The narrow walls pressed in around them until the group reached a second door—this one with a glass window that looked into a lobby area. She used the keys to unlock this door, too. "I only feel comfortable taking a handful of qualified students down here."

He didn't miss or appreciate the slight emphasis on the word *qualified*. It sounded like she was smelling dog shit as she said it.

"Where'd you dig up this freshman?" Devon Kurtwilder asked. He was directly ahead, and Cal nearly ran into him again as they all waited for her to unlock the lobby door and go through.

"Second-year," Cal corrected, irritable.

So much for making the best of tonight.

"Mr. Erickson is . . . a special case. For now he can just observe and pick up some of the preservation techniques we use," Professor Reyes explained. "An eager mind is always welcome."

"Pft. *Erickson*." Devon swung around, glaring at him with dark-green eyes. "Now I get it."

Cal didn't bother defending himself. His throat tightened up—from the dust, he decided, and not from humiliation. The door opened with a sudden, cold scrape, and Cal jumped. Professor Reyes held the door open for the two girls and Devon, but she stopped Cal, holding him by the elbow of his checked shirt.

"You'll have to forgive Devon," she said in a whisper, but her eyes and her tone never softened. "He, Maria, and Colleen have completed several grueling prerequisites to get down here and work on the preservation firsthand. You can understand if they're a bit . . . touchy."

"I get it," Cal said, taking his arm back. "And I can't blame them. Hey, if it improves morale, I'm more than happy to zip right back up those stairs and—"

"Nice try. Let's get moving; we're wasting time."

The other students waited in the lobby, their flashlights bouncing off the dusty surfaces of desks, low side tables, and abandoned chairs. It looked like a volcano had erupted, leaving everything covered in a thick layer of gray powder. Cal's nose itched and his eyes burned from the stale air.

"Maria and Colleen usually work together, so you can join Devon in room three."

Room 3. That sounded simple enough. Cal flashed his new partner a quick smile, but Devon had already turned down the corridor leading away from the lobby. Cal hurried to follow, suddenly afraid of being left without the light.

"And Devon?" The professor's needling voice echoed down the hall toward them. "Be gentle with him, and remind him of the rules, please."

Room 3 was small, little more than a cell, with a hanging metal lamp that had long since burst its bulb. The one high window was so grimy it didn't seem possible that any light could have made it in even in the daytime. Bars striped the glass, and the dirt from above had eroded, trickling against the window and gathering there in uneven mounds. It was impossible to forget that they were in a basement—he could feel the subterranean cold seeping through the worn soles of his shoes, chilling him completely.

"So," Devon said absently, kneeling next to an ancient, rusted cot. "The rules . . ."

"Sorry you had to get the tagalong," Cal replied. He let his eyes trail across the filthy walls and floor and then back to Devon's hunched shoulders.

The other student rummaged in a leather messenger bag, pulling out a notebook, camera, and a few pens, as well as a pair of white felt gloves. "Just don't touch anything, all right? That's rule number one for you."

Devon had a thick New York accent, though time away from home had rubbed off the rougher edges of it. Cal said nothing, watching him scribble something on his legal notepad. Then Devon grabbed the flashlight and stood, turning in time to reveal Professor Reyes just outside the door. She knelt, setting up a battery-run light on a little pair of yellow plastic stilts. It looked like what construction workers might use at night.

The lamp came on and Cal threw up his hand, covering his

eyes from the harsh glare.

"Happy hunting," Professor Reyes said, her eyes lingering on Cal before she disappeared again.

Happy hunting. Like anything could be happy in this room.

"She was talking to me," Devon said. He had moved closer to the cot, carefully peeling up the rotting blanket on it with his gloved fingers. "You're just here to observe for now."

"Thanks, I sort of picked up on that." Cal crossed his arms, absorbing the withering look the other boy tossed over his shoulder.

"Oh, good. A smart-ass. Can you at least take notes?"

"What do you want me to write?" Cal asked, taking out his own notebook and pen.

7:05 p.m., he jotted down. *Stuck in dank cell with sexy dickhead. FML.*

"I'll let you know when I find something," Devon muttered. Then he fell silent, absorbed in his work. Cal liked him a lot better that way. Tall, blond, with those dark-green eyes and lantern jaw . . . Not that it mattered. It was obvious Cal wasn't even a blip on the edge of Devon's radar. For the second time that evening he felt the invisible barrier rise; always on the outside looking in, just watching. Just an observer.

Well, screw that.

Cal turned to his right, wandering away from Devon's careful inspection of the cot. The room wasn't any less unsettling for the light of the work lamp. That lamp bleached the color out of things, turning the brown walls to a faded-photograph gray. How was this considered psychology stuff and not archaeology? What were they even hoping to turn up? A small table leaned against the wall opposite the cot, but there was nothing on it.

This room was empty—couldn't they see that?

Then Cal noticed something the work lamp had illuminated. He checked to see that Devon wasn't watching, then approached the wall. The thing that had caught Cal's eye was behind the little table, and he had to crouch to see it, squinting past one spindly leg.

It was writing—one cramped line of uneven text, scratched or carved into the concrete.

Ghosts, ghosts in the shadows, ghosts in the light, and now I am become one too

Cal stared at it for a long moment, hardly noticing that his hand had lifted pen to notepad and begun copying the words. His pen moved across the paper almost of its own accord. Then he felt a sudden cold breath against his left ear and, just as quickly, the absence of cold, of heat, of any temperature whatsoever, as if the air surrounding him had been sucked away.

He felt something. There. Just there next to his ear and slightly behind . . . Like someone was leaning over his shoulder, watching him write. His hand trembled, making a mess of the last word—*too*—the final *o* trailing off as if the letter itself had collapsed into a gasp.

"Hello?"

Cal froze. It was a little boy's voice, soft and curious. He craned his head to the left, and for a brief flicker he saw the boy's face, hovering beside him. Young—nine or ten—and his face was kind, but something was wrong with his head. It was lumpy, misshapen, as if he'd been in an accident.

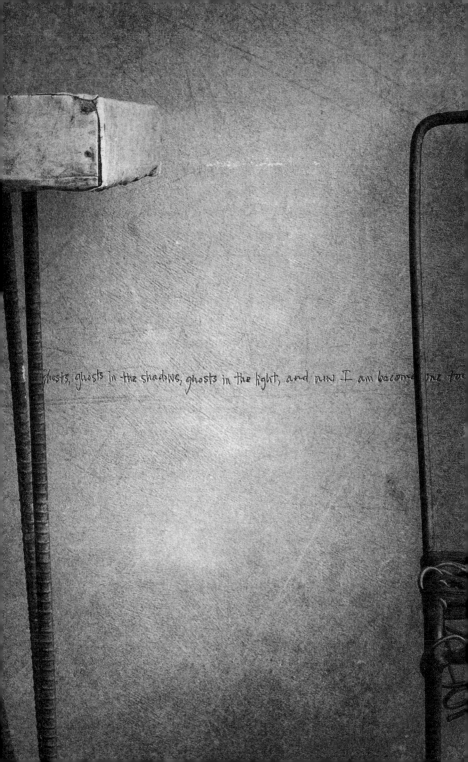

ghosts, ghosts in the shadows, ghosts in the light, and now I am become one too

"Are you here to help? Or are you like them, too?"

Cal shifted away from the face, the voice. It wasn't just his hand that had lost feeling now but his entire body. Cal jerked toward the door, his back hitting the wall. He had to get away. But the instant he moved, the pale little face vanished, and the scant warmth of the room returned. The light shone brighter, and Devon . . . Devon was staring at him.

"Did you say something?" Cal whispered. The face . . . The *thing* . . . It was gone, wasn't it? Or it had never been there to begin with. He searched the room, but there was nothing out of place.

"What's up? Did you touch something?" Devon stood, rounding on him. "I told you not to touch anything!"

"I didn't!" Cal inched toward the door, nearly tripping over the lamp. "I heard . . . You *really* didn't say anything? It's not cool to mess with me, man. It's creepy down here!"

"Professor!" Sighing, Devon tucked his hands against his waist and shook his head. "The newbie is spooked. You better get him out of here before he has a meltdown!"

That was just fine with him. Cal showed himself the door, plunging out into the corridor. It wasn't any better out here. He couldn't remember what it was like to take in a breath and not taste sour air. At least he could feel his hands again, and his feet, though he couldn't banish the feeling that that little boy was somewhere nearby, watching him. Watching him struggle to shove his notebook and pen away. Watching him struggle down the hall toward Professor Reyes, who bustled up to him with her brow furrowed.

"Is this some stunt of yours to get out early?" she asked,

drawing up too close for his liking. "I am trying to help you, Cal. I am trying to be patient and work with your father—"

"It's not a stunt," Cal said. Didn't he look pale to her? He *felt* pale. "I heard something. I *saw* someone."

Her brow relaxed and she took his arm, gently, leading him back toward the lobby. "You do look pretty shaken. All right, you can be dismissed early tonight. Get some air, Cal. It can be intense down here. I'll just need to search your bag first."

"Fine. Take it." He pushed the bag at her. *Whatever gets me out of here fastest.*

Cal watched her rifle through the bag, look over his open notebook, pause, and then put it back. She closed the clasp on the bag and handed it back across to him.

Down the hall, he heard a commotion as a door snapped open. He turned, seeing the faint glow of a flashlight come nearer, bouncing along the corridor. It was one of the girls. She skidded up to them, out of breath, pushing a feathery fall of brown hair out of her eyes.

"Professor," she said, glancing nervously at Cal and then back to Professor Reyes. "In the office . . . You should come look."

The professor's beetle-black eyes glittered up at Cal in the semidarkness of the corridor, and then she was waving him along. "You're free to go, Cal. Breathe. See your friends. Get your head together, because I expect you back tomorrow night."

By the time he had taken his next step, she was already vanishing down the hall.

CHAPTER

5

*H*e tried everything he could think of to get to sleep.

Micah didn't return to their room that night, and so Cal left his desk lamp on until long after midnight. He couldn't close his eyes without seeing the boy's face hovering there in front of him. When he turned on his side, his spine ached; when he turned on his back, his neck hurt. . . . What was wrong with him? He didn't believe in ghosts or hauntings or any of that crap. But he had seen something. He'd *heard* something. If he didn't believe that, then he didn't believe himself.

Cal rolled out of bed and stalked to the fridge, rummaging around until he found a travel-size bottle of vodka in the back. He downed it in one, sputtering and wiping at his mouth, then tossed the empty bottle into a Chinese takeout bag near the sink. Recycling. Close enough.

Back in bed, he didn't feel any more clearheaded. He closed his eyes. *No.* The boy was back, watching him, not menacing but *curious.* Curious was somehow worse.

Cal's pulse refused to slow down. He remembered this feeling from finals week last semester, when he was under so much pressure and stress that he'd stopped sleeping altogether. He would lie in bed and put his hand over his chest, and he would feel his heart racing out of control, unable to shut himself down, unable to turn off his brain. He felt that again now—that terrifying sense that he wasn't in control of his body or his mind.

He sat up, deciding to use his nervous energy to read and take notes. But he couldn't focus. Finally, he gave up and fished Fallon's comic book out of his bag. He stared at the pages until his next memory was of dreaming.

The little boy was there, in his dreams, just a blur of white and blue, following him.

"Are you here to help?" the little boy asked. They were holding hands now, walking down the concrete path on the quad outside Brookline. Cal could see himself holding the kid's hand, but felt no pressure, no warmth. . . . "Or are you like them, too?"

Cal couldn't answer. He couldn't control himself in the dream, and even if he could, he wouldn't know what to say. The boy pointed to the buildings around them, those that ringed in the grassy area of the quad. They were all in black and white, torn apart, the buildings streaming with particles as if they were dissolving slowly. And they were upside down, roofs bleeding into the faded grass.

"There are always two deaths," the boy continued, "the real one and the one people know about."

When Cal tried to look at the boy, really look, the boy would always turn away, sometimes twisting unnaturally, only ever showing the one small glimpse Cal had seen in room 3.

The rest of him was a blank.

"There's a . . . a *man* associated with the Bandar," the boy said, pointing at Cal. "Not a man, really, more like a phantom! A ghost! A ghost who walks, cannot die, centuries old . . ."

Cal looked down at himself. He was wearing a purple spandex suit.

What the hell?

"She found something." The boy's voice was high and would have been sweetly childlike, except there was something empty and sad to it. "She found the key, she found him, and now they'll never leave. We won't ever leave, we will just all go down together."

The boy stopped and looked up at him now, steadily. His eyes were black holes bleeding. "Are you here to help? Or are you like them, too?"

CHAPTER

6

"*C*al?" He was still dreaming, maybe. Something hard bit into his shoulder, rocking him from side to side. "Cal! Jesus. Wake up, Cal. Are you hungover again?"

"No. Shut up." Cal groaned, rolling onto his back and pawing Micah away. "Just . . . Didn't sleep well. Stressed. Roger is on my back again."

"Remind me to get him a ladder," Micah said, chuckling and drifting over to his side of the room. He dropped into his desk chair and watched Cal struggle to sit up.

Cal rubbed at his puffy eyes and reached for the water glass he usually kept on the bedside table. It was empty. He swore and slammed it back down.

"You can ask for that ladder the next time you two are chumming around," Cal muttered.

"What are you talking about?" Micah asked, leaning forward in his chair. He took off his glasses, cleaning them on the bottom of his polo shirt. Was he trying to grow a *goatee*? That had to be Lara's doing.

"I saw you and Roger in the quad the other day," Cal said. He carefully eased out of bed, taking his cup to the sink across the room to fill it with tap water. "Chat about anything in particular? Like his deadbeat son?"

Micah laughed, loudly, putting his glasses back on. The goatee certainly made him less nondescript, more of the dark and tousled bad boy Lara no doubt wanted him to be. "Contrary to popular belief, Cal, the world does not revolve around you. No, we were talking about some program he wants me to run. There are a few kids he thinks might be getting into trouble with townies off campus. He wants me to talk to them about my time in juvie."

"Funny, he didn't ask me if I wanted to attend."

"Probably because he wants to help you out himself," Micah replied. Cal could hear the growing exasperation in the other boy's voice. "You know I'm no fan of Roger, but where I come from, if your pop's in a position to help, you take it and you stop complaining about it."

"Where you come from, people eat *alligators*, so you'll understand if I don't jump to take your advice."

Micah put up his hands as if to surrender. "Suit yourself, man. I just think you're going about this all wrong. Let Roger help you out. Get on his good side and then he'll leave you alone."

Cal's phone jittered, vibrating across his desk. Wincing, he went to collect it, knowing before he even picked it up who would be messaging.

"Speak of the devil," he mumbled.

"Roger?"

"Who else?" He rubbed at his temples and the bridge of his nose; then he remembered that was Roger's tic and stopped.

"You know we're worried about you, right?" Micah said, but Cal wasn't listening. "Lara and I both are. You can talk to us if you need to."

"Yeah," Cal said. "Yeah, cool. Thanks."

My office. Now. I know you don't have class until noon, so no excuses.

"I'll probably take you up on that," he added absently.

He wouldn't, of course, but it was nice to think someone cared.

Cal loaded up his bag for the day and lugged it across campus. It would be Roger's office for a check-in; then Elementary Econometrics, which he actually looked forward to; lunch; that damned lit class; Intermediate Microeconomics; and then tutoring with Fallon. At least if he was busy, he thought, it might keep him from thinking too hard about the night before.

Roger's offices were in the prettiest building on campus, Middle College, the tall, tapered, nineteenth-century mansion not far from Wilfurd Commons. Bright, scholarly pennants hung down around the doors, which were always left open during days with good weather. The chapel bells finished chiming as Cal half jogged across the stone courtyard. A pair of senior girls passed, bringing a strong whiff of coffee as they went.

The light inside the building was cave-like compared to the pure, bright sun in the quad. Dark, wood-paneled walls lined the upper floor, with portraits of previous deans and presidents leading up to the row of office doors. Roger's was third, with a neat little nameplate and everything. Some of the other doors were decorated with college stickers or news clippings, but Roger's was fittingly austere.

Cal knocked, feeling his gut twist up into preemptive knots.

"Come in."

Deep breath. You can do this. You went to tutoring, you went to help Professor Reyes. You're playing along. You're playing along.

CHAPTER

7

*R*oger sat perched on the edge of his broad mahogany desk, his foot dangling weirdly, showing a sliver of red business socks. Gray pin-striped suit. Pocket square. He must have had fancy meetings scheduled. For a while he just studied Cal, pinching his lips up and then relaxing them again.

"Are you depressed?"

Cal blinked. "What? I don't know. Probably. Isn't everyone?"

Clearly that wasn't the answer Roger was looking for. He reached back on his desk and picked up a piece of paper. His office was just as devoid of personality as his door—his walls were blank except for a few college posters, touches of humanity probably added by staffers and not Roger himself.

"I have an email here from Professor Reyes," Roger announced, waving the paper around. Cal groaned inwardly. "She said you showed up on time last night—good, good—and then you 'grew agitated and insisted on leaving early.' Care to explain?"

"Did you seriously go to the trouble of printing that out?" Cal asked.

"I'm not rising to this today. I simply refuse to." He put down the email and clasped his hands loosely in his lap. "What do you want, Cal?"

That wasn't a loaded question or anything.

"What do you want?" Roger repeated, squinting. "I know it's not to make me happy, that's obvious. I don't know if you're still acting out because of the divorce, or because of your *identity* crisis, or simply because you lack ambition and focus, but I will know what you want. Think long and hard about that. What do you want?"

Cal shifted, staring down at his Top-Siders. He would rather be yelled at, or even hit again. He didn't know how to deal with this side of his father. "I . . . I don't know what I want, all right?"

"The sad thing is that whatever it is," Roger said, his voice dropping a little, "you could have it. We have the means. *I* have the means."

Roger stood, taking the email from Professor Reyes and a chunky fountain pen from his desk. He walked these things to Cal, holding them patiently. "Write it down, Cal. Write down what you want."

"What, now?"

"Yes. Now."

God, this was embarrassing. Cal took the paper and pen, flipping over the email, but not before glimpsing a stray sentence.

If you need your son to wake up, you know what to do.

Did everyone think he was beyond help? From where he was standing, his life really didn't seem that bad, but maybe he just couldn't tell. Whatever, he could humor Roger, who was clearly off his nut if he thought he could just—poof!—conjure what Cal wanted out of thin air. It was a stupid exercise, but probably harmless. Hopefully harmless. Swallowing around a lump, he flattened his palm and tried to write as if he believed that, surprised by how quickly the words came out.

I want my friends back. I want Devon Kurtwilder to notice me. I don't want to be
a screwup anymore.

He shuddered. Maybe this was a bad idea. Did he really want
Roger to know *anything* about him? Roger took the pen and
paper, reading it over and making a quiet grunting sound. He
glanced up at Cal, and for once he wasn't scowling. "This gives
me hope, Cal."

"That makes one of us."

His father laughed, drily, and folded the paper, tucking it
into one of his interior suit pockets. "What do you think of
Fallon Brandt so far?"

"Huh?" That was a leap. "My tutor?"

"Yes, Fallon. What do you think of her?" Roger took up his
perch on the desk again, studying Cal closely.

Diplomatic, be diplomatic, even if you have to channel Micah.

"She's . . . cool, I guess. Seemed smart. I like her."

Where was this going?

"Strange little girl, don't you think? I don't like her at all.
Keeps trying to break into secure networks on campus and
snoop around. It's probably nothing, but we can't take these
things lightly." Roger adjusted his tie, then smoothed it down
fussily with both hands. "She's a hacker, Cal. She's trouble.
She's rooting around in college archives for a lark, and I don't
like it."

His tone was icy again.

Cal started and stopped his answer a few times. "I don't get
it. *You* hooked me up with her. I thought I was getting help with
my English essay."

"Yes. I always prefer to kill two birds with one stone when I can," Roger said, smiling mildly. "But now I have this," he added, patting the pocket with Cal's list, "which means plan A it is. You do something for me, and we get you what you want."

We?

Cal laughed. He had to—this was absurd. Since when was his father at all interested in giving Cal what he wanted, instead of just forcing him to do what Roger himself wanted? "Unless you secretly have mind-control powers, that'll be kind of difficult."

Roger smiled and leaned across his desk to open a drawer on the other side. After a moment, he withdrew something small and glassy, the greenish surface reflecting the sunlight streaming through his office window.

"We're at a crossroads, Cal," Roger said, beckoning him over with an eerie look in his eye. When Cal looked at his father, he didn't see so much of himself anymore. He didn't recognize this man. "You take this and plant it somewhere in Fallon's dorm room. You do that, and things will be different. Better. I promise."

Cal drifted across the carpet, hesitating. He saw the little glass cylinder in his father's hand and felt his heart plummet. It was a pipe, and not for smoking tobacco. If he put this in Fallon's room, he could get her into all kinds of trouble. . . .

"She already has two strikes for tampering with college security," Roger continued, holding out the pipe. Cal stared at it, feeling his hand twitch. "One more strike and she won't be a problem anymore."

"A *problem*? And this is how you handle a problem? Roger, I don't want to get her kicked out," he said, feeling suddenly like a child, naive. "She seems nice."

"I'm sure she does *seem* nice, Cal. I'm sure she seemed very nice when she was trying to solicit your help breaking into my computer."

Cal flinched, and Roger smirked.

"Just as I thought. She's trouble, Cal. And the last thing you need is more trouble." Cal closed his fingers around the pipe, but Roger didn't let go, yanking him closer. "So I'm asking you, politely but *firmly*, to come to the other side. If you really want what's best for you and Ms. *Seems Nice*, you'll say yes."

The pipe came free and Cal stumbled back a step. His eyes flicked to Roger's pocket, where his list was hidden.

"If I don't do it?" he whispered. His lips were painfully dry.

"There are others currently on the right side who could go right back to being in trouble." Now his tone wasn't ice but steel, and when Cal met his father's eyes, they pierced. "Micah, for example."

Cal's fingers turned into a fist around the pipe. "He spent a few weeks in juvie for theft—who cares? It's not even that big of a deal. Nobody would expel him for that."

"Theft?" Roger's head hung back as he laughed. "Is that what he told you?" His laughter died down, and then the steel was back in his gaze. "You're even more out of touch than I thought."

Roger stopped there, but Cal refused to give him the satisfaction of asking for an explanation.

"Fine," he said. "I'll do it your way, then. Just . . . I don't want Fallon to get in too much trouble."

Roger waved him away, turning to pick up a mug of coffee

from his desk. His smile was back, as if this was business as usual. "You just worry about upholding your end of the bargain"—he tapped the list in his pocket—"and let me worry about upholding mine."

CHAPTER

8

My paunchy old man is in the collegiate mafia, Cal thought, dragging himself across campus to Fallon's dorm. All day the pipe had sat like an anchor in his pocket, a heavy reminder of what he was supposed to be doing.

Sure, he didn't *know* know Fallon, but she seemed decent enough. Not really in his social circle, maybe, but that didn't mean she deserved to get kicked out of school. Some of her tutoring had sunk in, and hadn't she let him borrow that comic book?

A comic book he had left in his dorm room accidentally. *Damn.* He would have to find a way to get it back to her, and hope that it could happen before an RA found the pipe in her room.

He passed the fraternity and sorority houses lining the road that led to the residential side. Cal watched the lights come on in the Sig Tau frat house, an old Victorian monstrosity with four white columns and a sandy brick facade.

Devon was probably inside playing Xbox with his frat brothers, telling stories about the underclassman who'd geeked out in Brookline's basement like a little baby.

Something brushed Cal's wrist. He looked down, expecting a bit of stray spiderweb or a bush frond, but it was that damn kid, smiling up at him.

The boy was holding his hand.

Cal gasped and jerked his fingers away from nothing at all.

The ghostly little boy was gone, leaving behind a whisper of cold on his skin. God, and he would have to go back inside that basement in—he glanced at his watch—three short hours.

But first, Fallon.

Cal hurried his steps to Jeffreys. He used the closer entrance, brushing past a guy who was ignoring the ten-foot rule and having a cigarette by the door.

There were elevators in the main lobby, but Cal took the stairs just inside the door. His footsteps echoed up all three floors, and music and soft laughter bled through the walls. In one room someone practiced the violin.

He made his way to Fallon's door and knocked under the plastic dry-erase board. He saw that someone had left her a note in green marker.

Hey Fal, stopped by. Miss ur cute fais. Check the subreddit, k?—Holly

And above that, in curlicue script: No Admittance Except on Party Business.

Cal knocked again, leaning in and calling through the door, "I'm not on party business, but we had a session scheduled."

He heard the latch go, and the door opened a second later. Fallon didn't greet him, so he elbowed his way inside, sighing and letting his book bag droop down to his elbow. The damn thing had to weigh fifty pounds with all his textbooks crammed inside.

The room smelled strongly of incense, which was against the

rules, but Cal was way past thinking this girl cared about the rules.

"Sandalwood?" Cal asked, nodding toward the brown stick smoldering away near the open window. She had used an empty soda can for a holder, wedging the incense stick through the tab. "Trying to cover something up?"

"Like what?" Fallon asked, giving him a blank look.

"Never mind."

She had already laid out the books and notebooks on the desk for them. Cal joined her at the table, sliding into his chair with a grunt of relief.

"Long day?" she asked. She wore a dark-blue sundress over shiny patterned leggings. Today it was a chain-mail necklace instead of a bracelet.

"You have no idea." Cal pulled out his copy of *Wide Sargasso Sea* and his notebook, opening it to find that message staring back at him.

Ghosts, ghosts in the shadows, ghosts in the light, and now I am become one too

He slammed the cover shut and leaned his elbows on it.

"You seem edgy. Want a beer?" She was already on her way to the mini-fridge.

"You sure that won't get in the way?"

Fallon shrugged, bouncing the messy curls on her shoulders. "My job is to make sure you pass your lit class. I'm not your sobriety coach. Here, I'll join you."

Stop being nice, you're making this harder.

"I got a good start on my essay last night," Cal lied, cracking open the beer she offered. It was ice cold, and he had to admit, it helped the jitters in his stomach. "So thanks. I think this is helping."

"Miracles really do happen," she joked, raising her can in a toast. Then she browsed through her copy of the novel, trying to find where they had left off. "Your dad still giving you a hard time?"

More questions about Roger. Maybe his father was right about her, and the friendliness was all an act. Cal shrugged, glancing around her room, looking for a spot to hide the contraband. "You know that basement in Brookline?"

Taking another sip of her beer, Fallon nodded and then picked up a pen, tapping it on the open book in front of her. "You got to go down there, right? What was it like?"

"Gross. Dusty. Depressing."

"So not a prime make-out spot then?" Fallon smiled and plucked at the tab on her beer can. It made a sharp twanging sound. "I'll scratch it off the list."

Cal blanched. "Oh, I'm . . . not really into girls."

"And I'm not really into guys." She winked, but it was friendly, and the jitters leaped again in his stomach.

He had to distract himself or he would come clean and tell her what his father was up to. "There was this part of the book I really liked. . . ." Cal searched frantically through his notes. "This line—'There are always two deaths, the real one and the one people know about.'"

Fallon nodded, her turquoise eyes suddenly distant. "Yeah. My favorite was always: 'Blot out the moon, pull down the stars.

Love in the dark, for we're for the dark so soon, so soon.'"

"You know that by heart?" Cal asked, impressed.

She shrugged and went back to her book. "Some things just stick, you know?"

He ran his hand over his notebook. He did know.

Cal reached into his pocket and shifted the pipe closer to his leg, farther in where he wouldn't be tempted to reach. It would stay hidden, where it belonged, and Fallon would stay at NHC, where she belonged.

CHAPTER

9

*C*al was feeling pretty proud of the fact that it only took two more beers before he had the courage to keep his appointment with Professor Reyes and the others. He arrived promptly, if not eagerly, clutching his book bag and a flashlight of his own.

Tonight I won't touch anything or even look too hard at anything, he promised himself. *I'll stand still, I'll watch what Devon does—which is really not such a bad way to pass the time—and that will be that.*

But they were a man down when he arrived—specifically a *Devon* down.

Immediately, Cal thought of the folded piece of paper in his father's suit pocket. *This isn't good.*

Just a coincidence, he assured himself. Devon was an athlete; he probably pulled a muscle in the weight room or took a bad fall in practice.

"Where's Devon?" he asked, sticking his hands in his pockets and eyeing the two girls, then Professor Reyes. He had left the pipe back in his room, locked in a combination safe under his bed.

"It's disappointing, but Devon won't be joining us," Professor Reyes lamented with a heavy sigh. "And since he was your

supervision, that means you're off the hook for this evening, Mr. Erickson."

"Oh," he said blankly. "Bummer."

"Yes. I'm sure you're *devastated*."

"I'll be going, then. . . ."

"But we'll be seeing you tomorrow evening, the usual time." Professor Reyes took out her key ring and turned away, finished with him. "Girls, I want to start in the office right away today. If you find another mention of that boy, you bring it to me. No need to make copies of anything, just bring me the originals."

Cal didn't dare let out a relieved breath until he had cleared the corner and was already bounding up the stairs. Devon's unexplained absence was weird, but probably nothing. Cal's relief was cut short, however, when he arrived back at his room.

He could hear the commotion through the door.

"This is BULLSHIT."

Micah. Micah didn't yell. Micah never raised his voice above a low Southern drawl. This was—

"Who told you?" he was screaming now. "Who told you!?"

Cal peered inside the door, afraid something would come hurling toward him if he busted in too quickly. His roommate paced the border between their halves of the room. The phone clutched in his white-knuckled fist looked like it was about to shatter.

"You couldn't tell me this in person? You had to fucking text me?"

Cal could hear a high, frantic voice on the other end. A girl's voice. He wedged himself farther inside, feeling his pulse crank up a few notches as he fit the pieces together. They were fighting,

breaking up again, but this was sooner than he expected. Usually they at least lasted for a few weeks. . . .

"I'm not that person anymore," Micah was saying, calmer now but still with that hint of breathless desperation Cal had never heard before. "You know I'm not that person."

Finally Micah noticed Cal and swiveled around to face him with wet, shining cheeks.

"Is everything okay?" Cal mouthed silently.

"I have to go," Micah said into the phone, hanging up and throwing it savagely at his bed. It skipped across the mattress, bumping against the pillow. "She broke up with me," he said in a hollow whisper, staring at the floor as if he had never seen it before. "Again."

The next morning, the goatee was gone.

CHAPTER

10

I'm disappointed, Cal.

*T*hree little words. Cal's thumb hovered over the phone, but he didn't know how to respond. He hadn't planted the pipe, and now he was left to hope that Roger had been bluffing about the potential fallout of his failure.

I just need more time, Cal finally replied.

That was a lie. He wasn't going to do it. Somehow, he would have to fix this. He would just have to go to Roger's office and call the whole thing off, promise to do better, *be* better, with no bribes or threats on the table.

Whatever was going on between Fallon and Roger, that was between them. And really, all luck to Fallon. Maybe she'd find something in Roger's emails to put him in his place.

Cal set his phone down on the mattress. Slashes of early morning sun peeked through their curtains, and he splayed his hand in one of the patches of light on the blanket, feeling the warmth on his skin—the opposite sensation of the little ghost boy's hand.

He shuddered. That dream had come again. This time the boy had been with him in Brookline, leading him down to the door that could only be opened with the professor's keys.

"Go through," the boy had said, pointing. "Go through, ghost who walks, go through."

That was all Cal could remember of it. He drifted in and out of his morning routine in a haze, forgetting to brush his teeth before stumbling out the door with Micah still dozing in his bed. Cal texted Lara to see if she was doing okay and received an immediate—if negative—response.

He had his friends back, but not the way he wanted them.

His class load was lighter that day, which was good, considering he would hardly be able to keep himself awake even with an energy drink. After his last class, he had his final tutoring session with Fallon before his English paper was due.

He jogged past the frats and sororities to Fallon's dorm. The dark clouds that had been gathering all day looked ready to burst, and he didn't want to add soaking wet to exhausted, confused, and stressed.

He checked his phone as he took the last few stairs to her floor, surprised to find Roger hadn't dashed off an angry response to his text. It wasn't like Roger to take failure this quietly.

Frowning, Cal glanced up from his cell to find he wasn't alone in visiting Fallon. A petite girl with neon-blue hair was waiting outside the door. One side of her head was shaved, and the rest was gathered up in a haphazard ponytail at her nape. The oversize tank top she wore hung off her bony frame, showing a lacy pink bra underneath.

She turned and looked Cal up and down.

"What's your story, pretty boy? You looking for Fal, too?"

"She's my tutor," he said, curling his lip. "Who's asking?"

"Holliday." She stuck out her hand. Her skin was so pale it

was almost translucent. Every knuckle sported a ring of some kind. One of them even looked hinged, like she could hide something inside it.

"Cal," he said. They shook hands, and her fingers were like ice. "Is Fallon not in?"

"Not in. Not answering emails. Not answering her phone." Holliday shrank a little, pressing her palm to Fallon's door. "Fal doesn't do that. She doesn't go dark, not without telling me first."

Oh shit.

"Maybe she's just hung up in class," Cal suggested. "Reception blows on the academic side."

"It blows here, too, but her phone's boosted. Look, I don't know why I'm telling you this, pretty boy. Just holler if you see her, okay?" Holliday jerked him closer by the arm. She was surprisingly strong. She yanked up his sleeve and produced a black permanent marker, scribbling her number on his forearm.

"Hey." He pulled his arm back. "You could ask first."

"Yeah, whatever. If you see anything, you text me." Holliday shoved away from him, glancing at Fallon's door one last time before slinking down the hall.

If I see anything. What if I already know something?

Cal almost messaged Roger to let him know his tutoring session had to be canceled, hoping against hope that Roger would respond with surprise. But he had a strong suspicion that Roger already knew. That he had found some other way to remove his so-called *problem.*

No, no, no. This couldn't be happening.

CHAPTER

11

*C*al didn't go straight back to Brookline. He wandered around campus, hoping that a solution would come to him, or that he'd run into Fallon, who would explain that she'd just been asleep in the library or working out at the gym. Maybe her phone had died, and she'd completely forgotten about their tutoring session. Eventually, Cal headed back to his room, convinced that he was being paranoid and there were any number of logical explanations for where she might be.

When his phone finally buzzed an hour later, it wasn't Fallon or Roger. It was a number he didn't recognize. Cal read the message with the feeling that his whole world was turning upside down. Any other day he would've welcomed this surprise. But today, after everything, he stood in the middle of his room, staring at his phone in mute horror.

Hey, this is Devon. From the other night? We got off on the wrong foot. We should meet up tonight. Maybe grab dinner?

"How did you even get this number?" Cal muttered at the phone. He blinked hard and wiped at the sweat starting to prickle at his temples. Okay. This could still be fixed. All of it could be fixed. First, he would take that stupid pipe back to Roger. He would calmly explain that he didn't want any part of what was happening here—that making the list at all had been a mistake. Cal didn't care about any of it—didn't want anything from anyone.

He certainly couldn't go to dinner with Devon. Not yet. Not until he knew just what the hell was going on. That lame platitude, "Be careful what you wish for," flashed mockingly in front of his eyes.

"Yeah, yeah," he mumbled, going down on his knees to search under the bed for his lockbox, "I'm an idiot and this whole thing is my . . . fault."

He stopped. The box was open. That couldn't be. . . . It had a six-digit combination. *Micah* didn't even know he owned it, and they were roomies. Cal pulled the safe out, scrambling to see what was missing. Just the pipe.

Of course.

"New plan," he said decisively, but he could feel the heat rising in his cheeks, the familiar knot of panic twisting up his insides. The phone in his pocket chirped loudly, and Cal almost fell back down to the floor in alarm. "Jesus, you're losing it, Erickson."

The message had come from another unknown number. Not Devon this time, but someone else.

Look outside your window.

He was sweating in earnest now, almost to the point where he couldn't keep a firm grasp on the phone.

Cal threw himself toward the window.

There was the new girl, Holliday, standing down in the quad with her electric-blue hair glowing under the pathway lamps. She held her phone to her ear with one hand and the pipe above her head in the other. Then she lowered the phone, obviously typing something.

Missing something?

Forget the stupid phone. Cal shoved the window open, leaning down to shout, "How the hell did you get my number!?"

Holliday pocketed her phone and the pipe, though how she fit them in her skinny black jeans he could not tell from here. She pointed at the window and mimed marching. So she was coming up. Lovely.

"The room's not really in a state for company!" he yelled down to her.

"So what!"

Cal leaned back and slammed the window shut. He didn't trust Holliday even a little bit. The freak had somehow managed to break into his dorm room and crack his safe. She was probably a hacker just like Fallon.

His phone jumped in his hand again, this time with another text from Devon's number.

Cal? Did you want to get dinner? Don't leave me hanging here, man.

Yes. No. Goddamn it.

It almost felt good, liberating, to grit his teeth and type back.

Not tonight, Devon. Maybe some other time.

CHAPTER

12

"*I* just blew off dinner with the hottest person I have ever seen in real life," Cal fumed, stomping across the room to the door, "so this had better be good."

"Correction: hottest automaton you've ever seen," Holliday said, closing the door resolutely behind her. "Here," she said, tossing the pipe to him. "I knew that would get your attention."

"There are easier ways," Cal told her hotly. "Like the phone, for example. Or a cordial email! How did you know the combination to the safe—seriously?"

She wandered around the room, glancing into picture frames and picking up random items as if she had been there a million times before. Who knew, maybe she had. "Now you know I'm not messing around."

"Messing around about what? What do you want from me?"

"It was your mother's birthday," Holliday said, leaning casually against the window and crossing her arms. She blew a puff of slushie-blue hair out of her eyes. "Which I got from your laptop, the password to which was your favorite musician, whom you have a poster of above your bed." She glanced at the Jack Johnson poster and rolled her eyes. "Who is frakking terribad, by the way."

Frakking? Terribad? "What are you—from the moon?"

"No, the Internets." She smirked. The space between her nose and lip was pierced, just a little silver stud like a mole. "Which is how I got your phone number. Fal and I share everything, and whenever she tutors someone new, she gives me their number in case something goes wrong. Precautions."

"You do that?" Cal asked, lifting a brow. He didn't know what to do with the pipe in his hands, so he tossed it awkwardly onto the bed and prayed an RA didn't stop by.

"We're girls. Of course we do that." Holliday rolled her eyes as if this were the most obvious piece of information. "Anyway, I still haven't heard from her. She's gone. Missing. I know she is. And I know they took her."

"They?" This was getting crazier by the minute. But if he thought it was crazy, why was he still sweating bullets? "Who are *they*?"

"The spooks who run things around here," Holliday said, taking out her mobile and touching the screen a few times before showing it to him. On it was a picture, blurry, of two figures running by. They were dressed head to toe in red, capes maybe, their faces hidden and turned away from the camera. "They. Them. The Scarlets."

"Aren't they just some academic fraternity?" Cal had heard of them, but in the loosest of terms. Allegedly only the smartest kids from the "best" families were invited to join. He had one of those things going for him, not so much the other.

"If that's what you think, then they're doing their job. At first Fal thought you might be one, too, but after meeting you she was convinced you're clean," Holliday said. She stepped over to his desk and slumped into the chair, wheeling herself closer to

wake up the laptop. Without a hitch, she typed in his password.

Cal grumbled, making a mental note to change it.

"Personally I'm shocked you're not one of them."

"Maybe I am," he said with a snort, "and you just don't know it."

The desk chair squeaked as Holliday swiveled to turn and face him. She lifted one slender black brow. "Yeah. I'm not buying it." She turned back to the computer. "You're no Scarlet, but your daddy is."

"My . . . ?" Cal joined her at the desk, leaning onto it and over her shoulder. "What are you talking about?"

But the twist in his guts had turned into something solid, an icy pool that grew and grew, heavier and harder to bear by the second.

Holliday typed furiously, opening a browser and then several new tabs. "That pipe—you were going to frame Fallon with it, right?"

Cal hesitated, which was answer enough for her, apparently.

"That's what I thought. The administration has been trying to get Fallon and me kicked off campus for the tiniest infractions for two semesters now, and the pipe would have been Fal's third strike. But you didn't plant it." Here she stopped again, tilting her head to the side to stare at him. She had dark eyes, almost black, and a tiny pointed chin. "Why *didn't* you plant it?"

Cal shrugged. "My father kept saying Fallon was trouble and that she was hacking into his stuff. That doesn't mean she should get booted off campus. Hell, she should get a medal for it."

"He's right. As far as he's concerned, she is trouble. So am I.

Last year our friend Michelle got weird. Like *really* weird. We thought maybe she was just going straight-edge or something, but then she stopped talking to us, even looking at us. We'd try to wave at her, right? And it was like we weren't even there. So . . . we might have gone digging in her email. Not great, I admit, but we were curious." Her fingers flew across the keyboard, and Cal watched as she brought up the Internet gate for the college archives. "Watch this, okay?"

She started running various searches, some on "Brookline" and "asylum," others on "the Scarlets" and "society," then more on "Camford disappearances." Few results returned. The articles on Brookline were brief, he could tell, and seemed more like cheery blurbs meant to placate worried parents than actual historical documents.

"And now this," she said, opening a new tab and typing a URL that jogged his memory.

"Didn't you write something about this on Fallon's door? About a sub-something?"

"Yeah, this is our subreddit," Holliday explained, giving him a quick, approving smile. "Good catch. After we busted into Michelle's email, we couldn't really stop looking. There's way more here. This guy?" She pointed to the screen with a chipped black fingernail, showing Cal the handle $4UL. "He's got news clippings from the last forty years, plus pictures, theories. . . . But none of this stuff is in the college archives, and whenever Fal or I try to hack them, the encryption is ridiculous. We are talking military levels of security, and why?"

Cal couldn't tell whether she expected an answer or not. Either way, hacking wasn't exactly his expertise. "Maybe because

they stored some of the asylum patient files there for posterity? They might not want people looking at those for privacy reasons. Professor Reyes seemed pretty protective of the files in the basement."

"I think there's more. I think there's way, way more. And we're going to find out." Her eyes gleamed, suddenly brighter and less black in the glow of his desk lamp.

"Shouldn't we be trying to find Fallon?" he asked, pushing off from the desk and ruffling his hair. "That seems like the more pressing issue."

Holliday stood, too, slinking over to him on her spindly legs and grinning up at him. A little crazy, maybe, but he wasn't going to mention it.

"We're not going to find her." Holliday turned to glance at the pipe abandoned on the bed. "*You* are."

"Me?" Cal looked down at his own shirt, as if maybe she had mistaken him for someone else. "What the hell am I supposed to do?"

"You and your dad solid?" she asked.

"Solid? No, not exactly."

"Well, you'll just have to fix that when you text him," Holliday said, rolling her eyes.

This was all moving a little fast. "Text him about what?"

"We have to record your dad admitting he's involved in the Scarlets, and that it's not just some innocent academic thing," she said. She rummaged in her tiny pockets again, coming up with her own phone. "I can hide nearby. You just have to get him to explain how he tried to frame Fallon. Can you do that?"

God, maybe he should've taken Devon up on that dinner

invite after all. But he was way past that, wasn't he? He had to know if Roger really was responsible for Devon asking him out. For Micah and Lara breaking up so suddenly. For Fallon falling off the grid . . .

"How does this help Fallon?"

"If we can get him to admit something shady, then we can turn it back on him," Holliday said, biting her lower lip. It didn't exactly inspire him with the greatest confidence. "Blackmail the blackmailer, you know?"

Cal sighed and glanced toward the window. "You really think this will work?"

"He's just a man, Cal," she said, squaring her frail shoulders. "He's just your dad, yeah? Don't forget that. He's just your father."

CHAPTER

13

I t might technically have been spring, but Cal was freezing as he waited in the quad outside Brookline. Holliday wasn't far, probably just as cold as she watched him from a clump of trees and bushes a few yards away.

I tried to put the pipe in Fallon's room, but she won't answer the damn door. Suggestions? Can we meet to talk about this?

He narrowed his eyes, irritated by the too-bright screen of his phone and the message on it. He hadn't been sure that Roger would even respond to his text. But Holliday had urged him to send it, and now that he had his father's answer, he had to admit that her whole skull-and-crossbones conspiracy thing was starting to feel less like a conspiracy and more like reality.

I'm coming to you. Meet me outside in twenty minutes.

The quad was empty except for Cal. He noticed a shape moving across the courtyard farther along toward the academic side, and then the silhouette resolved into a man roughly Roger's size. A thin fog drifted across the grass, swirling against the base of the tree where Holliday lay in wait.

81

Cal watched his father march closer, reassuring himself that he had not just seen that pale wisp of the ghost child flicker in Roger's wake. He waited, and trembled, and revised his list in his head: *I want my friends to be okay, whether they're dating or not. I want Fallon to stay at the college. I want to tell her that I liked the comic book. . . .*

"Good," Roger said, slightly out of breath as he finally approached. He glanced around them, then took Cal firmly by the elbow. "You're here. That's good. Come on."

Cal followed with faltering steps, feeling his arm bruise under his father's grip. "Come on where?"

He didn't want to get too far from Holliday and her phone. If Roger really was guilty of abducting someone, they needed him recorded and in his own words.

"Inside. You may have failed to uphold your side of our bargain, but you know too much. You're one of us now."

One of us?

"One of who?" Cal asked. They were going back inside Brookline, and Cal's chest filled with a dull ache, a roar, a blood-deep warning that something was very wrong. "What's going on? Where's Fallon? She's not in her dorm, and she's not answering her phone."

"God, I really did raise an idiot," Roger muttered. "But at least you're finally cooperating."

Cal's mouth went dry. He heard soft footsteps behind them and silently begged Holliday to stay back, to not get too close to this, whatever this was. This wasn't part of their plan, and he didn't want her and Roger to end up in the same room together. In his gut he knew where they were going, and he stumbled after his father on unsteady legs as Roger led him to that alcove, that basement with its damned giant lock.

Roger withdrew his own key, a single one, from his trouser pocket and fit it into the lock.

"Why do you have a key for this place?" Cal whispered. "What the hell are you mixed up in, Dad?"

Chuckling, Roger glanced down at him and then hauled him bodily through the door. "You must be truly frightened to call me that."

"Not frightened," Cal said quickly. He had to play the charade and convince his father he was on his side. *Think.* "I just had no idea being a Scarlet gave you access to so much."

That gave Roger pause. He nodded, slowly, making a thoughtful sound in the back of his throat. "It gives you access to *everything*, Cal. This college—this town—is the Scarlets. But you'll see."

Increasingly, Cal was certain he didn't want to see.

"The Brandt girl was close, oh, she was close. And sneaky. I'm guessing she and her friend aren't the last of the fools snooping around. We haven't taken care of them all yet, and we might never, but by God, we can send them a warning."

"Who are you talking about?" Cal tried to keep his voice even. "You sound paranoid."

"Not paranoid, just prepared."

Cal's throat itched from the dust as they descended to the lobby and the basement level. He heard voices, scratching sounds. He hoped again that Holliday would stay back.

"Why didn't you tell me about this sooner?" Cal asked, honestly curious.

Roger let go of him, seemingly satisfied that Cal really was

there on his own terms. They moved through the snowy softness of floating dust motes, leaving behind the lobby and entering the corridor Cal was familiar with. The scratching and voices grew louder, and he heard a solitary laugh like a flutter of wings in the dark.

"I told you, I like to kill two birds with one stone when I can."

Roger showed him his teeth, not a smile exactly, but a flare of the lips, a tasting of the air. Like a predator. An animal.

Cal heard the voices grow louder, though they never rose above a constant, monotone mumbling. Roger stopped outside room 3 and took Cal by the shoulders, making him stare up into his face.

"This means you'll be one of us now, son," Roger told him solemnly.

Cal blinked and tried not to run. It was finally sinking in that he already *was* a part of this. Whether or not he had meant to end up here, he was going to be part of whatever was in that room. He hadn't stopped it, and maybe that made him as bad as the rest.

Just stay back, Holliday. Stay out of this.

"Now," Roger said, squeezing his shoulders and giving a true smile, an ecstatic smile, "let's get this problem sorted."

Firmly, he guided Cal by the shoulders into room 3. It was just like Cal remembered—the crumbling walls with their spreading stains of damp and mold; the tiny, lightless window; the forlorn little cot and table. . . .

But there was more there now, a chair, sturdy and new, with cuffs for the arms, legs, and neck. Fallon was in that chair, struggling against her bonds.

Cal could feel the little ghost boy there, watching, *accusing*.

"I'm not here to help, am I?" he murmured, his chin trembling suddenly. *"I'm like them, too."*

"What did you say?" Roger asked, but he didn't wait for an answer. "Never mind that." He raised his voice, turning slightly and calling toward the door. "Get the other one. She was scuttling around in the shadows behind us."

Footsteps, a pair of them, clattered down the corridor. Then Cal heard a cry—Holliday's—and not a moment later she was being wrestled into the room by two cloaked figures. They were wearing red robes. Cal shuddered, feeling his father's grip on his shoulders tighten.

"Let me go!" Holliday was thrashing, fighting. "You psychos! Let me *go*! You can't hurt me." Her tone was rising and getting desperate. "You can't hurt me!"

Roger laughed softly. "Down here we can."

Fallon stared at Cal from her bonds in the chair. The brightness had gone out of her turquoise eyes. A swatch of duct tape kept her mute, but he could hear her trying to shout behind it.

"I do not think Ms. Brandt will go hunting for secrets anymore," Roger was saying behind him. "No, she and her friend were always trouble, always meddling. Meddlesome girls can find themselves poking into dark corners where they don't belong." He lifted his hand, swiveling to indicate room 3 and the basement beyond. "Like this one. Such girls might, say, fall down a rotted staircase. Get lost. Disappear."

Disappear? What did he mean, disappear?

That invisible barrier, the one Cal hated but knew like a friend, was gone. He was here, really here, and the full feeling

of being present was almost too much. He feared now, and hated, and he wanted the barrier back. He didn't want to feel this.

Cal glanced up, holding back another wave of nausea. There was the chair with Fallon in it, and a figure beside her all in black. Next to them was a table with strange medical instruments. . . .

"Calm down," Roger barked, turning to Holliday. The robed figures were still trying to subdue her. One of them finally managed to get a strip of tape across her mouth. But Holliday had seen the table and the tray with the shining, sharp instruments. She fought harder, tossing. "Those aren't for you, not if you behave yourselves and do as we say."

"We?" Cal wrenched himself out of his father's grasp. "I have nothing to do with this! This is all you, you and your Scarlets, with . . . with this!" He pointed at Fallon in the chair. "So what if they were hacking you? Expel them, I don't know, but Jesus, just let them go!"

"You said he was with us." It was the figure in black speaking now. The voice sounded familiar, feminine but dampened by the mask. He couldn't quite place it, and now he didn't know where to look—Holliday was being dragged out of the room, kicking and tossing, and that black-robed figure was advancing on him, holding up a long, silver spike, like a pick.

"Calm him down," she was saying. "Or I will."

"No need for that," Roger said, putting up his hands. He approached Cal slowly, carefully. "I thought we were all on the same page, son. I've upheld my side of the bargain, have I not? I've given you everything you wanted."

Cal laughed, crazed, and crouched low, trying to find a way out. He couldn't get around his father, and that shiny silver spike was getting closer. . . . "I don't want *this*, you sicko! Who do you think I am?"

"I have no idea," Roger said gently. "And that's exactly why you're a problem."

Cal saw his father nod. Was that a signal? Behind her gag, Fallon cried out, warning him. Cal spun, seeing the black-robed figure appear right behind him, that spike in her hand. More footsteps echoed down the corridor. They were done with Holliday and coming for him. He would be swarmed, outnumbered.

He didn't think. Cal lunged, grabbing the spike and twisting it out of the stranger's hand. Then Roger was on him, trying to yank him down to the floor. With a furious grunt and all of his strength he spun and threw himself at his father. Roger stumbled back against the doorway, too slow. He recovered fast, aiming a punch for Cal's gut that never connected. Cal swung, arcing his arm over and down, slamming the spike into his father's eye.

Cal felt the blood hit his face, sudden and warm, and he stumbled back, sickened, maybe blind. Was there blood running in his eyes? He couldn't tell. . . .

Fallon stopped shouting behind the tape.

Something came down hard on his head, splintering his vision and knocking his legs out from under him. He could hear his father screaming, thrashing, and the blood on Cal's face grew sticky and thick.

There are always two deaths, the real one and the one people know about.

The world went black and then gray, shifting and breaking apart, streams of particles that he watched bleed together. Like the upside-down buildings. Like his phantom dreams.

His father went on screaming as a shadow fell across him, the last dim image Cal saw before the darkness swallowed everything.

"It's all right. We'll get this cleaned up." It was a soft voice and low. The figure in black. "You're one of us now, Cal. We'll take care of you. We'll take care of everything."

THE
BONE ARTISTS

Man's main task in life is to give birth to himself, to become what he potentially is.

—ERICH FROMM, *MAN FOR HIMSELF*

Calamities are of two kinds: misfortune to ourselves, and good fortune to others.

—AMBROSE BIERCE, *THE DEVIL'S DICTIONARY*

*T*hese were the rules as they were first put down:

First, that the Artist should choose an Object dear to the deceased.

Second, that the Artist feel neither guilt nor remorse in the taking.

Third, and most important, that the Object would not hold power until blooded. And that the more innocent the blood for the blooding, the more powerful the result.

Prologue

*H*is friend's voice was frantic on the other end of the line. Oliver had only heard him that upset one other time, when they had climbed a nasty old chain-link fence in Bywater and Micah had sliced his palm open on a jagged link at the top. The cut clearly needed stitches—there had been blood soaking Micah's clothes, all down the front of his new Saints T-shirt. The blood was on Oliver, too, but somehow he remained calm, got Micah to pedal on his bike back through the neighborhood toward home. Then came Micah's grandmother and a trip to the hospital, and it was all fixed.

Oliver wasn't so sure any phone call or hospital could fix this. He could hear something sizzling and popping in the background, and his friend could barely breathe as he wheezed into the cell phone.

"Ollie? Ollie, oh shit, I'm so sorry," he said. "I'm sorry, I'm so, so sorry. . . ."

Chapter 1

Four Days Earlier

*O*liver splashed his face with ice-cold water, reaching blindly for the hand towel he knew would be hanging just to the right of the mirror. He didn't bother with a shave, since he was growing attached to the wiry scruff of a goatee he had managed to grow. Hey, at seventeen that was a badge of honor. It wasn't nearly as full or legit as Micah's, but that kid was descended from swamp people, and from the pictures Oliver had seen at Micah's house, even the youngish cousins all seemed to have giant shag beards, messy as birds' nests, by twenty.

And anyway there wasn't time to shave. He had to pick up his girlfriend, Sabrina, and Micah from karate or judo or whatever they were teaching at the dojo where they worked.

Oliver dried his face, smirking, patting down the wisp of a mustache over his upper lip, trying to hide the scar that subtly deformed the skin there. A surgery for cleft palate as a kid had left him up one scar and his family down a significant load of cash. He hated hospitals. What was the point of insurance if they could still gouge the hell out of you for stuff like surgeries? On a kid? It was all backward.

That was one of many reasons he daydreamed about hauling ass to Canada one day. Things were different there. Oliver could get far, far away from his family's shop and do something, maybe open a garage. Tinkering with cars for the rest of his life would be just fine, especially if Micah and Sabrina came along. Was Vancouver nice? Or Ottawa? He'd have to look it up. They could try Montreal, even though only Micah spoke a lick of French, and his was the muddled Creole kind.

But Oliver was getting ahead of himself. He had news. Awesome news. Sabrina and Micah needed to know ASAP because Oliver was bursting out of his skin trying to keep it to himself. He hurried out of the small bathroom, avoiding the creaky old door that never shut properly anyway. Katrina had done a number on the building, and the lingering damage had left the doorways, floors, and ceilings warped. Most of the doors in the house had to be shouldered shut because of misshapen wood frames. Without the cash to make the repairs, Oliver's family had seen only to what was most crucial—the active leaks, the windows broken by looting, the mold, the water-damaged furniture. . . .

He winced, thinking about all the small fixes he would do if he had the time. Or hell, the money. That would change, he decided. Not right away. Not with the minimal cash flow he managed between working hours at the family antique shop and the Part-Time Job.

That's how he referred to it in his head. It was easier to pretend it wasn't shady—wasn't *illegal*—if he gave it a nice, safe nickname.

That Part-Time Job would be taking up most of his Monday evening, but for now he had that news to deliver and breakfast

to snag on his way out the door. Spring break was a godsend. Prime tourist time, it meant his father was busy almost nonstop in the shop—knickknacks of the vintage variety were always big with visitors to the Big Easy, and the flow of tourism seemed to get better and better every year. It had been scary there for a while in the recovery years, but now things felt almost back to normal. That thrilled his father, and it thrilled Oliver, too, since it meant he could pick up as many hours as he wanted now and also feel better about leaving his dad later.

Because he was definitely leaving. Finally, the University of Texas had gotten back to him. Missing the early decision deadline had stressed him out big-time, but now he had his answer and the answer was: yes, Oliver could attend the school's mechanical engineering program. Hell, maybe if things went his way he wouldn't just tinker with cars for a living, he would *design* them. Austin was close enough that Oliver could zip home for any holidays or family emergencies, and it was far away enough to escape the long, long shadow cast by Berkley & Daughters.

The family business. Oliver could hear said business booming next door. The Berkleys liked to keep work and home close together, their second-story suite of apartments just one door and two dozen steps away from the shop.

Correction—Nick Berkley liked to mingle business and family. Oliver wasn't in love with the shop the way his dad was.

"That's what I told your granddaddy, too," Oliver muttered under his breath. His father had informed him as much the last time they'd had the same old dinner conversation about Oliver's future. It always ushered in a tense silence. Forks and knives were never so loud screaming across plates.

Oliver opened the closet, grabbed a light canvas coat, and pulled it on, patting the pockets to make sure the acceptance letter from UT was still there. Its reassuring bulk on the left breast gave him a smile. Dad didn't know yet, and frankly, Oliver wasn't eager for that confrontation. But screw it. Today was about feeling good. It was about spring break.

The closet was wallpapered in news clippings, magazine pages, and posters, some glossy, some faded. It was like a living timeline of his life and interests—flaking LEGO ads taped over with Catherine Zeta-Jones posters taped over with cheesy fantasy dragon illustrations taped over with muscle cars taped over with Saints pennants. An odd little time capsule to hold his simple wardrobe.

The corridor leading from his attic-like bedroom down the hall to the kitchen was narrow and dark. Nobody smart had designed the layout of the apartment—the halls all turned out pokey and far, far away from any natural light. On the kitchen counter, the last two bananas were about to go bad, so Oliver took them both, peeling one and pocketing the other as he grabbed a bottle of water out of the fridge.

Coffee would come soon, but not until he had Sabrina and Micah with him. Then he could push the crisp, white paper across a café table to them and sit back to sip his morning brew with everything just a bit righter in his world.

Chapter 2

*H*e didn't expect her to call on his way to pick up Sabrina. Oliver pulled his beloved Challenger over, idling it safely against the curb, too nervous to juggle the phone, banana, and steering wheel all at the same time. Not with her on the line. Not with her voice slithering into his ear.

"Oliver, dear, it's been six whole days. That's practically a lifetime in my line of work," she said.

Sucking in a deep breath, he tried to let the hum of the vintage engine put him at ease. This was just a phone call. At least Briony the Dragon Lady wasn't sneering down at him in person. Christ. That was an experience he dreaded with every cell in his body.

He tossed the half-eaten banana into the passenger seat. The almost too-ripe smell was making his stomach go queasy.

"Hello, Briony," he said with singsong mock enthusiasm. "Good morning to you, too."

"Do I need bloody cheek from you? No, I certainly do not."

The first time Oliver had met Briony Kerr, balanced on her knife-dagger high heels, he had made the mistake of thinking her attractive. Objectively, she was, but the wife of his boss was all angles—blunt cut, peroxide-bottle white hair; frosty-gray eyes bearing down on him like lasers. . . . He shuddered at the most recent memory. A six-day-old memory, in fact.

Oliver watched the tourists going up and down the sidewalk. "We're finishing up tonight. You'll have what you asked for tomorrow, all right?"

Shit. Tomorrow. In the wake of his good news, Oliver had managed to push away the thought of the Part-Time Job he and Micah needed to finish that night.

"I see. Tomorrow, then."

"Yup!"

"You're lucky I'm such a patient woman."

Patient! What a crock of . . .

"So lucky," Oliver chirped. "The luckiest."

"Right. You can dispense with the sarcastic commentary, Mr. Berkley. I'll expect to see you at seven tomorrow at your family's *charming* establishment."

He waited until the other end went dead before releasing a huge sigh. There was no telling if it was from relief or irritation. Oliver chucked his phone onto the passenger seat and eased his car back out onto the street, wary of the heavy foot traffic that tended to spill over into the roads. Chewing the edge of his thumb, he did his best not to gun the engine and smash into a few pedestrians. It might have helped his mood. Then again, he was already flirting with the wrong side of the law by working for Briony; the last thing he needed was anyone looking too closely at his after-school activities.

His phone buzzed on the seat and Oliver swept it up, keeping one elbow balanced carefully on the steering wheel. It was Sabrina's ringtone.

Don't tell me you have to cancel, he thought.

"We finished early," the text read, "meet u at CC's."

That suited him fine, since the crosstown drive to grab them from the dojo and get back to CC's was a pain. But from where he idled at a stop, it wasn't far to the locals-only coffee joint on Esplanade. Finding parking was a nightmare, especially for a muscle car, one that didn't exactly fit the sizing standards of the narrow old New Orleans streets. An honest-to-God thundercloud hovered over his head by the time he pushed open the door to the cafe and inhaled the bitter, exhilarating scent of fresh coffee grounds.

That early in the morning and that frustrated, he could bathe in that *smell*.

Oliver swung his keychain around his forefinger while he waited in line, eyes focused on nothing in particular. He knew what he wanted, but his mind kept drifting unhelpfully back to their impending obligations.

From the start, Oliver had kept Sabrina out of it. She knew what he and Micah were up to, but only in the sparest sense. It was Micah who'd pulled him into it in the first place, some family connection through one of the kooky old swamp dogs related to his friend. At first it seemed like a joke. Dig up a few musty pocket watches for extra cash? Sure, count him in. It wasn't all that different, after all, from what his own family did at their antique shop.

He rolled his eyes at the thought. All right, that was pushing it. There were, of course, unethical people in the salvage and antiques world, but that wasn't how the Berkleys operated. They didn't steal, they didn't swindle, and they certainly didn't rob graves.

God, but Oliver hated putting it that way.

He just had to keep Sabrina out of it and hope that while she and Micah taught the kids classes at the dojo, Micah never spilled more than was appropriate.

You're robbing graves together for the Dragon Lady, none of this is appropriate.

"How ya doing today?" Grace, the girl behind the counter, practically pierced his eardrum with her greeting. She beamed up at him, knuckles to the countertop, wiggling like she was at the start of a race.

Nobody should ever be that cheerful at this hour. . . .

"He's grumpy, apparently, Grace, so you better make it a double shot Americano today." Micah had crept up on him, clapping a hand roughly on Oliver's back. He yelped and jumped, shooting Grace a sheepish smile. *Damn karate-jiu-jitsu-ninja skills.*

"Yeah," Oliver agreed. "What he said."

"The usual for you two cutie pies?" Grace asked, turning her same bright smile on Micah and Sabrina. They had changed out of their teaching clothes, but still looked like they had come from working out, Micah in a loose gray tee and track shorts, Sabrina in a Lycra sport top and sweatpants.

"That'll do nicely, Grace," Micah said, turning on the charm. He matched her smile, leaning onto the counter by the register and winking. "When are you going to go out with me, Grace? It's just not fair."

"Oh, you big fool, stop teasing." Grace rolled her eyes, shaking her head of thick, red ringlets before passing their orders on to another barista. "Y'all been teaching this morning? Aren't those kids in their little white outfits just the cutest darn thing? Melts your heart."

"You should come around sometime. You know, take a class. I could show you. . . ."

"Mega gross-out," Sabrina muttered.

That was Oliver's cue to take her aside, away from Micah's hot pursuit, and clear of the line forming behind them. Customers were already grumbling about the holdup. Fit and tall, clean smelling even after teaching kids karate all morning, Sabrina always made him feel like a slouch. The luckiest slouch. It felt like sheer, dumb luck that she even went out with him. Micah had introduced them a few months back and somehow it all just clicked. It had been a rare stroke of romantic genius to pick her up in his Challenger, take her to Raising Cane's to grab some chicken fingers to go, and then perch near the river on a bench.

They'd talked until it was dark and angry texts started pouring in from her dad.

Months later, the smell of french fries and Texas toast still made him think of that afternoon and made his heart beat a little faster.

"You need to talk to Micah," she said, shattering his olfactory stroll down memory lane. "He's being a total shithead about Diane."

"Diane?" Clearly he was a few steps behind. "Is she ticked at him or something?"

"No! Oliver, come on, baby, you know where this is going. It's *Micah*."

Oh. *Oh!*

"Yeah okay, I can see that . . . that it would be weird for him to go out with your sister."

"Practically *incestuous*, okay?"

"Well, hey, slow down, no . . . We're not brothers or anything." Oliver was beginning to realize he had no leg to stand on in this conversation, as he himself found the idea of he and his best friend dating sisters to be *weird*. "But I take your point," Oliver finished, and he was rewarded with a brief flicker of a smile from his girlfriend. "I'll talk to him."

"Thanks, baby." She leaned in and kissed his cheek, then breezed by to pick up the coffee orders that had just been called.

Damn. Already off on the wrong track for the day. It wasn't supposed to be about Micah. It was supposed to be about him. His news. His future.

Chapter 3

"Hey, so, I wanted to show y'all this," Oliver said, lurching up on his seat to take out his acceptance letter. He had finally yanked Micah away from the counter, luring him to a nice, airy table by the windows with the promise of good news. Fans whirred overhead. The bright, naked bulbs lighting the coffee house glimmered off the newly washed table.

Micah reached for the letter at once, grabbing it before Sabrina could get a look.

"Ass," she muttered.

"Oh, pipe down, would you? You'll get your turn."

"Yeah, but why you always gotta be first? What is with that? Compensating for something, big man? And what's all this shit with you and Diane? Don't think I didn't hear about that."

"*As I was saying,*" Oliver interrupted. He shifted his glass across the table, the soft screeching sound making his friends fall silent. "I got in. Austin. They said *yes.*"

"Hell yes they did!" Laughing, Micah thumped his fist on the table, shaking their cups. "That's what I'm talking about, brother. That's fantastic."

"Like there was ever any doubt."

Oliver cleared his throat, rubbing nervously at the scar on his upper lip. It felt good, real good, to get this kind of acknowledgment. Especially from Sabrina. God, he just hoped they could keep their relationship going when he moved away. Maybe she could come with . . . No, that was asking way too much. She had her own life to think about, and Austin wasn't so far away.

Sabrina reached over and touched his shoulder, smiling at him while Micah leapt up to buy them a round of celebratory chocolate chip cookies.

"Seriously, baby, I'm real proud," she said, rubbing his arm. She paused to take a sip from her steaming cup of coffee. She looked up from the mug and smacked her lips, gazing out the window, the bright sunlight making her smooth, dark skin glitter. "We should celebrate. I've got tonight free. What do you think? Cane's? Diane's got a fake ID, she could score us some champagne."

"'Cause we can afford that." Oliver chuckled and tossed his head.

"Just the cheap stuff, nothing crazy."

"And anyway, I can't," he said. "I promised Micah I would . . ."

I promised Micah I would help him rob a grave.

"That I'd help make gumbo for his church thing. He needs like three giant batches and it'd take him forever on his own."

"You two idiots don't know how to cook a good gumbo. I can stop by," she said with a shrug, but she had looked away, retreating a little. She wanted to celebrate and damn it, now Oliver had to lie to protect her.

It really is for your own good.

Briony and the others he saw sometimes at drop-offs never did anything, per se, but Oliver got the distinct impression they *could*. There was something unnatural, something *vicious* about that woman. Nobody ought to be able to walk in heels that high and that pointy without falling over. And the others? Well, they were worse, in a way, often so silent, just hunched over, working, working, scraping, *carving*. . . .

"Babe, you know how his people are," Oliver said softly, meaningfully, in the voice he hated to use, the one that always made him feel like he was naked and screaming at the top of his lungs.

"Ha. Yeah. His grandmother and black people. Just one more reason he should keep his crazy ass away from Diane."

"You know how he is when he gets an idea in his head," Oliver said, hiding behind his glass. Micah was on his way back to the table, cookie-heaped plate in hand, a smile on his face like he needed to seduce the whole world, including his best friends.

"Yes," Sabrina said with a sigh. "Yes, I do."

"I don't know why he'd listen to me over you."

"Because your bro-code bullshit has reached peak levels," she muttered. "And he never listens to me anyway."

"I'll talk to him, Bri, I promise. Tonight, okay? We'll have the whole night to talk, just two bros making gumbo."

Making gumbo. Robbing graves. What was the difference, really?

Chapter 4

"*Y*ou know, Briony called me today. She call you at all?"

Micah hurried along next to him, thumbs hooked into the straps of the backpack bouncing on his shoulders. "Me? No."

They both hunched over, heads partially obscured by dark hooded sweatshirts. Parking on Derbigny, they walked the rest of the way to the cemetery's entrance. A big, flashy muscle car sitting right by their destination wouldn't exactly have been subtle.

"What did she want?"

"She's impatient. She wants the Roland job finished. I'm supposed to drop everything off at the shop tomorrow. . . ." Make that *today*. Two in the morning. He'd probably look a tired mess, just grabbing a few hours of sleep before he had to be up and helping in the family shop. "I hate when she calls. It's like she can see me through my damn phone."

"Maybe she can."

Oliver swatted his friend on the shoulder, sticking close as they rounded the corner, following the jagged outline of wrought-iron fencing that outlined the cemetery. "Don't be an idiot."

"Who's being an idiot?" Micah threw a quick glance toward

the aboveground mausoleums rising like dunes in the darkness. "Oh. Of course. Mr. Skeptical . . ."

Oliver lowered his voice, checking to make sure nobody was following them as they neared the gates of St. Roch's. "What? You think she's a witch or something? That's farfetched, even for you."

"Not a witch, no. But ain't nothing wrong with having a healthy fear of what you don't understand."

"I understand that she's rich and that she has us by the balls until we get this done and she forks over the cash."

Any fear Oliver had of that woman was grounded in reality. She probably hid guns and worse in her fancy little blazers.

The entrance to St. Roch's stood guarded by two white statues, pious women with their hair braided around their heads like crowns. But Oliver and Micah weren't going in the conventional way, not when the gates would be shut for the night. They stopped well shy of the main entrance, stooping in the looming bulk of a crenellated brick building. Micah knelt and made a cradle out of his hands, helping Oliver step before hoisting him up, holding there until Oliver could scramble safely over the top of the fence. He landed with a thud, remembering to bend his knees to make for a softer descent. Micah climbed the iron bars with no trouble at all, practically a monkey from his years of athletic training.

Once inside, surrounded by waist-high monuments and graves, the boys fell silent. Oliver didn't believe in any of the old-school, mystical, Voudon junk Micah did, but graveyards spooked him all the same. The thought that there were bones everywhere beneath their feet, eyeless skulls watching them

just below the surface of the earth, spindly fingers crossed over their chests or at their sides, or reaching . . .

Micah smacked him on the chest, nodding toward the path to the left, and farther down that way, the chapel. Not a single tree broke up the line of sight between the gates and the chapel itself, giving the cemetery a stark, desolate feel. No oaks hung with moss and resurrection fern, just open air and the profile of the chapel rising against the moon and stars. Someone down the block had cooked barbecue that night, a smoky, tangy scent lingering over the graves. Oliver's stomach turned at the combination of cooked flesh and what he knew lurked below his sneakers.

His friend led the way, dodging nimbly around stone markers and mausoleums. By day, St. Roch's wasn't much cheerier, not in Oliver's opinion. It was an institution, and a kind of macabre mecca for Southern loreseekers. He had never been inside the place before, but Micah had. They swept clear of the front doors of the narrow, tall, white building, keeping to the right side. As they'd previously discussed, both of them stayed low, Oliver turning to keep an eye out for security guards or curious pedestrians on the sidewalk. The spring heat worked in their favor, coaxing most folks, even those keen for an evening stroll, to stay inside by a fan or AC unit.

Micah, meanwhile, did what he did best.

A latch clicked over his shoulder, and Oliver braced. It just seemed wrong, sneaking into a chapel, into a place of worship, poking around where people had prayed and where the two boys didn't belong.

Chapter 5

*O*r maybe just *he* didn't belong.

Micah held the crooked old window open long enough for Oliver to squeeze through and then slid in behind him, chuckling softly as he did so. Breaking in, sneaking around . . . It came to Micah as naturally as breathing. He had gotten busted for stealing little stuff when they were younger, a candy bar here, a CD there, but Micah always found a way to talk himself out of it and walk away with a slap on the wrist.

But that was Micah through and through, changeable with the wind. The good little church-going, God-fearing kid one week and the big bad influence the next. Oliver never knew which one would show up on any given day.

And without him you wouldn't be even close to affording tuition. Suck it up.

Two thousand bucks to dig around for a few pocket watches and necklaces was too good to pass up.

"Did you bring the list?" Oliver whispered. The chapel had to be empty at that time of night, but he kept his voice low all the same. Micah walked quickly to what looked like a low shelving unit and a bunch of lumps on the wall opposite from where they had broken in. His boots crunched over cockroach shells.

"It's in here," his friend replied, tapping his left temple. He pulled a box of matches from his pocket and struck a light, then leaned forward and touched the flame to a half dozen candles of varying heights scattered across the lowest shelf.

Oliver gasped as the room and all that was in it flared to life.

"Jesus Christ," he whispered.

"Kind of inappropriate, mm? Given the circumstances," his friend chided playfully. "Stop gawking, we have shit to take care of."

"Sorry, it's just . . ." *Horrifying.*

The word died on his lips but stayed vivid in his mind. The wall was covered in pieces of human beings, or rather, plastic and wood and glass parts of former owners. Prosthetics. Plaster feet, plaster hands, masks, arms, even glass eyeballs skewed and directionless, watching him under the warm glow of the candles. Most of the hands and feet hung from metal hooks pushed into the plaster.

A chipped, yellowed statue of Mary presided over the collection from a nearby corner.

"I'd heard about this place, just didn't realize it would look like this," he said, approaching the abandoned relics slowly.

Micah, meanwhile, had shoved his face close to what appeared to be a carved wooden peg leg. He squinted, peering over his glasses and twisting his head, trying to read something on its side. "Yeah. Freaky, huh? They're mostly just repros. Thanks for healing my hand, Saint Roch, here's a model of it. It's a little easier to swallow in the daylight."

Somehow Oliver doubted that.

Not that he was a stranger to odd artifacts—his father's shop was full of the stuff, little taxidermied raccoons and alligator claws and bird skeletons. . . . But there was something different

about these left-behind pieces. He reached out and, with trembling fingers, touched one of the smooth, white hands. He shuddered; it was warm to the touch, heated by the candles, but felt as if it had just been plucked from a living owner.

"So who was this Roland person anyway?" Oliver murmured, recoiling from the wall.

Micah didn't seem to mind doing the bulk of the work, searching along the wall for his target. "Does it matter? We just need to find his hand thingie and his fingers."

"Wait. Fingers? You don't actually mean—"

Snorting, Micah shot him a wry look, finally unhooking a plaster-cast hand from the right corner of the shrine. "Do you honestly think grabbing this thing off the wall is worth two grand to someone? Come on, Oliver. Use your head."

He felt suddenly queasy, watching Micah stuff the hand in his backpack, the open zipper revealing a sliver of a small garden trowel. The other boy leaned down and blew out the candles, leaving them abruptly in darkness, the shrine filtered through coils of smoke.

"I thought we were just taking *stuff*, not bones. That's messed up."

And it's not what I signed up for.

Micah crossed to him, his face hovering just an inch or so away, his eyes a dull, dark gray as they roamed over Oliver's face. Then he clapped Oliver on the shoulder and shrugged, nodding toward the jimmied window behind him. "I don't like it either, man, but do you honestly want to back out now?"

Immediately he thought of Briony, of getting on her bad side.

"These aren't good people, Ollie," Micah was saying, going to hold the window open for him to crawl through. "They do shit I do not agree with. There are forces they play with that guys like you and guys like me do not get. That we have no business trucking in. They ain't called Bone Artists because they carve *wood*."

Oliver nodded, pulling in a shaky breath. "I get it. I'm just not sure I can—"

"I'll do it," Micah told him in a soft, strange voice, pitying, maybe. "Just keep watch. It'll be slower that way, but at least we won't get caught."

Chapter

6

*O*liver was beginning to sweat heavily in his sweatshirt.

It was the humidity, sure, but it was also the sounds. He listened to the scraping of Micah's trowel as he dug out the corner grave in the cemetery. Try as he might, he couldn't drown out the sounds—the *shhesh-shhush* as Micah made piles of the displaced dirt, the louder breathing as the heat and the work took its toll, the sudden bursts of loud, cackling laughter from a house down the street. . . .

"Are you almost done?" It was a stupid question. Oliver wasn't foolish enough to think unearthing a coffin was a moment's work. He shifted, trying to stay low enough to blend with the gravestones and mausoleums. With no trees and little shadow, they were completely exposed to the night and to whoever might come looking.

That smoky, unsettling barbecue smell drifted over the cemetery, mingling sickeningly with the heat.

Micah said nothing, continuing to dig.

"Listen, I told Sabrina I'd talk to you about this Diane thing. She's not happy about it. Y'all are grown-ups and it's none of my business, I know that, but like . . . Don't you think with your family and everything it's just not a great idea?"

"I wouldn't exactly be bringing her around for supper."

"That's what I mean. Don't you think that's wrong?"

"Could you shut up? I'm trying to work here. . . ."

Oliver winced, turning to make sure nobody was watching them from the rear fence of the cemetery. Silence. Silence and then that sudden laughter and the smell of cooked, smoked flesh filling his nose . . . He tightened the muscles over his stomach, forcing down a wave of nausea. Closing his eyes, he visualized that two grand. He pictured getting his first tuition bill, setting up loans, trying to make this degree work with what little he could scrape together.

And anyway, Micah was taking the bullet, doing the worst of the work.

"Sorry," he whispered, wiping at the sweat pouring off his temples.

He rested his arm against the stone of a stout, rectangular mausoleum, feeling the stone gradually warm against his over-heated skin. With no trees there were no strange shadows to wreak havoc on his imagination, but without that cover he felt watched, and maybe he should. If all the mystic mumbo-jumbo Micah believed in was even half true then surely their actions were stirring up the dead.

Shivering even in the humidity, he grew still, hearing the trowel make a hollow cracking noise, bumping against more than dirt.

Micah mumbled something, maybe a prayer, and then Oliver heard a rusted latch giving way to metal snips. He had to wonder just how many tools of the trade Micah had in his bag; Oliver had never asked for a tutorial. If he knew how to break into a secured building or pick a lock, then he'd have no reason to bring Micah along on these jobs. He'd have to go alone, and that, he thought with a noisy swallow, was not an option.

He turned and knelt in the disturbed dirt heaped beside the grave. Micah hadn't dug very far. Oliver wondered if maybe the hurricane had left the graveyard with less topsoil and therefore less to cover the grave. St. Roch's had been under standing water just like everywhere else. The coffin was old, or maybe that was just what earth, wear and tear, and a flood did to a wooden box. Almost all of the other marked graves were above ground, corpses safely covered by stone or within the mausoleum itself, much smarter for flood country.

This grave, he noticed, wasn't marked at all.

"Are you going to keep watch or help?" Micah asked, out of breath. He jammed the trowel between the lid and side of the coffin, wiggling it.

The lid began to give and Oliver felt his courage waver. "Keep watch, I guess. Um, let me know if you need help."

But actually please don't.

He swiveled, closing his eyes again as the sounds continued, painting almost as vivid a picture as if he were watching the robbery itself. His mind filled with sudden doubts. He really should have read up on the penalties for getting caught doing this stuff. Was it better or worse that they were stealing from a dead person? No injured parties, really, but trafficking in body parts couldn't be nothing in the eyes of the law, either. Shit. Maybe he should have told Sabrina more about this. She was clever, clever enough to stay away from shady crap like this. . . .

But not clever enough to stay away from me.

"Bingo," he heard Micah whisper. There was another sound,

the worst one, listening to the quick, meaty chop as Micah severed the fingers from the hand. Flesh. Jesus, that meant the body couldn't be *that* old. Micah winced, trowel scraping along the bottom of the box as he scooped up the bones.

"This is so disgusting," Oliver hissed.

"There's no blood or anything."

"Not the point, man."

"I've got what we need," Micah said, ignoring him. "Let me cover this back up and we can—"

"Hey!" Oliver froze at the sound. It was a man's voice, loud and clear, calling to them from across the yard and back toward the entrance gate. "Hey there! Is someone there? What do y'all think you're doing over there?"

"Shit! Run!" Micah shoved the trowel and a plastic baggy into his backpack and took off running, closing the gap between the unearthed grave and the back fence of the cemetery.

Oliver tripped into a sprint, chest squeezing with sudden panic. They were caught. It was over. That guy would call the police and they would get picked up, bye-bye, Austin. . . .

"Faster than that, moron!" Micah whispered, dropping to his knee and motioning for Oliver to hurry his ass up. Oliver pumped his legs faster, listening to the man bang his fists on the iron gate, shouting at them still and getting louder. He didn't hesitate, grabbing the closest bars and using Micah's hands to vault over the tall, sharp points of the fencing. Micah landed beside him a second later and grabbed him by the sleeve, yanking him along a weedy, paved plot to cut diagonally back toward the car.

Was that a siren? Was his mind messing with him?

As they fled, Oliver took one last look behind him, breath lodging in his throat as he noticed the figure in the distance. Just a shadow, maybe, just a trick of the eye, but it looked like a tall silhouette stood over the unmarked grave, watching them run.

Chapter 7

*O*liver dragged his feet as he went to the back room. Six forty-five p.m. Briony would be there any minute to pick up the package. He shouldered the curtain aside near the register of the shop, vaguely aware of his dad trying to sell a customer on a refurbished coffee table. Ugh. Coffee. He could use a gallon right about then.

He hadn't slept. Not at all. When he'd closed his eyes he'd heard Micah's trowel hitting the coffin lid. He'd heard the fingers separating from the hand, so much severed meat. He'd heard that man shouting and the rattle of the iron fence. He'd seen the shadow watching them, right by the grave. Too close to the grave.

Sirens sounded all the time during the night in the city, but each siren that blared last night he'd been certain was coming for him.

Stifling a yawn, Oliver caught a glimpse of himself in an antique mirror in the supply room. Yikes. He looked dire. Scruffy was usually a good word to describe him, but this was something else. Dark circles rimmed his eyes. His hair stuck up, unwashed and oily, greased from the night spent roasting in his hoodie and sprinting for safety. He had stuffed his messenger bag next to a cabinet, hyperaware of what was inside of it.

Micah was teaching martial arts until close, leaving Oliver to do the hand-off. The first time around had been so much easier. Micah had deciphered the coded ad for fences on Craigslist and then they'd gone to the designated drop-off area to pick up an assignment in an old mailbox. That time they'd just had to pick up some watches, a pair of spectacles, and some other old junk that nobody would miss. Then they'd done the delivery in the same anonymous way.

The next time they answered an ad, Briony was there to meet them and showed them to what she called "an office," which turned out to be little more than an old garage in Bywater. Oliver had gotten the feeling that Briony certainly didn't live there and maybe didn't even spend much of her time in the dingy hovel. It gave him a distinct serial killer vibe, but a dozen or so people were there, busily working away at cramped desks. Oliver couldn't get close enough to see just what they were doing. At any rate, Briony had announced she was pleased with their work, and thought they might be good for something a bit more challenging.

Challenging enough to be worth two grand.

Oliver knelt and grabbed his bag, running his hand listlessly back and forth through his hair. It was over. They had done the work. He'd give the package to Briony and that, he decided, would be that. No more jobs. He didn't care how good the money was, it wasn't worth this stress.

It only remained to be seen if he could actually say all of that to Briony's face.

The bag vibrated in his hands and he fished out his cell phone. His dad never liked him to have it in his pocket while "on the floor." Two messages. One had come from Sabrina, another offer to celebrate his big news. The other was from Briony. He clutched the phone harder, a reflex.

Change of plans. Meet me by 8.

Directions followed. Oliver knew the place. It wasn't far at all. An easy walk, in fact. He debated taking the car, but figured he'd be able to get in and out faster if he made up some excuse to Briony about needing to pop right back to work, that this was his break and he needed to finish his shift.

He shouldered the bag and ducked by the curtain again, stepping out into the showroom of the shop. His dad was still working an old lady by the postcards. A few Tulane kids had showed up to set up tables and chairs for a poetry reading they were having later. Oliver mumbled hello to everyone, waving bye to his dad.

"Just gone for a minute," Oliver said, hoping it was true.

His father was almost a carbon copy of Oliver, longer in the face and with a few more wrinkles, but with the same shaggy dark hair and thick brows, same dark blue eyes and crooked smile.

"Where you headed?" Nick Berkley asked, jotting down a price offer for the customer on his little lined notepad.

"Just around the block. Didn't sleep much, need a coffee."

"We've got a pot in the back—"

"*Real* coffee."

His father shot him a mock-scandalized look and tucked his pencil behind his ear. "All right. Get back soon, okay? I want to talk about that big news of yours."

Oliver nodded, the door jangling shut behind him, the bells tacked to the frame announcing his exit. He wasn't sure that his sleep-deprived brain was ready for that talk with his dad. It had been a mistake to mention that he had news at lunch, but his mind hadn't been firing on all cylinders.

The city lamps had come on, washing the cobbled streets in pretty, welcoming light. Vintage light. It gave the sidewalks a surreal glow, something meant to give tourists that sense that they were stepping back in time, that none of this was real, that anything they said or did in their drunken journeys down Bourbon Street would be left behind in another world altogether.

No such luck, Oliver mused darkly. He'd be fortunate if he ever managed to scrub the night before from his mind. And even if he picked up and left for university, New Orleans would still be his home. That would never change. It had been a misstep to get wrapped up in this *Part-Time Job* with Micah.

For God's sake, this was his city, his *neighborhood*, and now he was traipsing across it with a guilty hunch to his shoulders, human bones rattling around in his bag.

Just as he thought, the GPS brought him to Briony's chosen spot after a ten-minute walk. A flashy, polished black luxury car was parked by itself on the block, the license plate reading PRNCPL1. A forest-green sticker with white type covered the bottom right of the bumper.

PROUD PARENT OF AN HONOR ROLL STUDENT

The rest of the street was mostly empty save for the odd lost, drunk tourist. By then the clammy evening humidity clung

heavy to his shirt, and he plucked at it to keep it off his damp skin as he double-checked the address, loitering outside of a wooden door down a soggy, sour alley.

He began to grow nervous as the minutes crawled by. Did he knock? Did he text Briony? Then the hinges of the door squealed and a face appeared in the gloom beyond, the stark white face of a painted mask.

Chapter 8

Oliver turned in a slow circle, gazing at the shelves upon shelves lining the walls of the facility. Facility? Office? He had no idea what to call it, but it was just like the last place Briony had told him to go, only this time it wasn't a crappy garage but a larger, multiroom apartment with tobacco stains yellowing the ceilings. The smell of cigarettes and cheap booze had steeped into the walls and floor, a scent that some kind of powerful cleaner or chemical was trying to overtake.

It was not a place that ought to be brightly lit, he thought, every sign of water damage, age, and decay showing starkly under the near-medical lighting. The Dragon Lady's crisp, cornflower-blue pantsuit was the cleanest thing in the room by far.

But just like in the garage, Briony didn't hang around the place alone. At the edges of the room, men and women bent over desks. These were sturdier and shinier than those at the garage. Oliver blinked, anxious, rocking on his heels while he waited for Briony to finish a phone call. The distinct buzz of a bone saw came screaming through a closed door to his left. The screech was like nails on a chalkboard, a cold sting zinging down his spine.

He couldn't overhear Briony's conversation, but he could hear the soft lilt of her voice. Not the tone she ever used with

him, not in person and not on the phone. He pulled off his backpack, and the weight of it—of what was inside of it—felt like a barrel of lead bricks.

Casting an eye around the room again, he tried to peer at what the closest desk person was doing. It was a man, and he wore rubber gloves, but that was the extent of his professionalism. His leather jacket and skinny jeans had him looking right at home among the grunginess.

Under the sound of Briony's voice ran a constant murmur of soft sounds. These were the Bone Artists—the actual ones—Micah had been going on about. He wondered if the fingers in his backpack would end up on one of those desks soon.

But for what?

Don't ask questions. This is the last time, remember?

Briony spun on one high heel, giving him an acid smile while she hid her phone in both hands, cupping her palms around it and taking a few clicking steps toward him.

Without prompting, Oliver thrust the backpack at her. He had already taken out his phone and anything valuable. She could keep the bag. He didn't want it.

"Eager to be rid of me?" Briony smiled. She didn't take the bag, however, waiting until the man in the leather jacket paused his work to stride over and grab the backpack for himself.

"I heard there were complications." She drew out the word, watching Oliver intently.

The bone saw next door grew louder. Oliver clicked his teeth together, clenching.

"We got what you asked for. Isn't that what matters?"

"Yes, but you were seen." She lifted a thin, arched brow. "Or do you not read the news, Mr. Berkley?"

Shit. He hadn't. Just getting down to the shop without dropping to sleep on his feet had been a chore.

He swallowed and gave his best nonchalant shrug. "We got away, nobody saw our faces."

"Are you certain of that?" The other brow went up.

Was this a trick question?

"Positive," Oliver said, beginning to sweat. "We took off before the guy could get close."

She nodded, her brows returning to a neutral position. Her entire face iced over, unreadable. He wished that damn saw would stop screeching next door, it was putting him on edge. *More* on edge. "So?" he prompted. "It's all there, right? We're square now."

"*Are* we?" She turned her head to the leather-jacket guy, who gave a quick nod. "Very good, Mr. Berkley. I think I like you." Leather Jacket disappeared for a moment into the room with the saw, the sound growing so loud with the door open that Oliver had to fight to keep from covering his ears. Muffled voices joined the racket and then Leather Jacket returned, replacing Oliver's backpack with a wad of bills held together with a rubber band.

"Try not to get into the papers next time, mm?"

Oliver blinked. "I don't think there will be a next time."

"No?" She stared at him steadily, a tiny muscle quivering in her chin. Then she smiled, but there was nothing behind it. Just teeth. Just a bright, white sliver carved across her face. "Not even, say . . . five thousand dollars could tempt you?"

Five thousand . . . ? *Jesus.*

"I can't," Oliver ground out.

She turned away, wandering with Leather Jacket toward the room with that infernal bone saw still whirring away. "Your friend might say otherwise."

"He might," Oliver allowed.

Briony's cold laughter chorused with the high-pitched saw, and Oliver's spine went rigid again. Her pale eyes caught him and snagged as she glanced over her shoulder. "I think you'll change your mind, Mr. Berkley. In fact, I *know* so."

Chapter

9

*H*e tapped out a manic rhythm on the steering wheel as he careened toward the dojo. His phone chirped every now and again on the passenger seat, alerting him to an unread text message from his father. Whatever guilt trip awaited him in that message could be kept on hold.

He didn't have the balls to face his father, not when he felt sick to his stomach. Five thousand dollars. That was more money than he had ever possessed at one time. Who was he kidding? The two grand in his dash compartment was hard to wrap his mind around, too. But this was grave robbing. It had to be way more illegal than taking a few family heirlooms. That made him feel crappy enough, but taking bones? Taking parts of *people*?

What were they doing in that creepy place anyway? So busy, bent over their desks, little worker ants going about their business so single-mindedly. His skin tightened just thinking about the possibilities. But that five grand would get him so much closer to his goals. . . . His fingers beat faster on the wheel as he waited for the light to turn. One more block and he'd be at the dojo. Micah might not have answers, but he would at least have sympathy and maybe a bottle of booze to make the whole thing easier to bear.

Micah's place of work didn't actually look *anything* like a dojo. It looked like the kind of blah storefront in a strip mall that might have once been a furniture warehouse or a doughnut shop. All but two windows were frosted over, but you could walk by and peer inside at whoever was chopping or kicking the air. Oliver was early—well, technically he wasn't anything, since Micah wasn't expecting him—and so two rows of little kids, swimming in their starchy white outfits, were still doing their best to punch at nothing under Micah's instruction.

Oliver pulled into the narrow parking lot and stopped the car under a flickering streetlamp. The electric glow of the strip mall was plenty, but some well-meaning city planner had tried to gussy up the place with cutesy benches and lamps, green, quaint, like there weren't a grimy tobacco store and an AutoZone in plain view.

He grabbed his phone and blanked out the message. He'd read it later, when he wasn't feeling so scattered. Sighing, he pulled open the dash compartment and took out the roll of cash, just holding it. Just feeling it. It felt heavy, and he knew exactly why. He shoved it back in the compartment and glanced up at Micah, wondering what two grand meant to the guy. Of course he had applied to colleges, too, some heavy hitters, in fact, but everything in Micah's life just seemed so breezy. So easy. His grades weren't the best but he usually got them bumped up by magical extra-credit projects wheedled out of exasperated teachers. He volunteered. He worked. His teachers could hardly blame him for missing an assignment now and again. Didn't make much money so he found a way to get more. Wink and a smile. Sure, they were essentially grave robbers now but it was two grand. Things would work themselves out.

Maybe Oliver could fix his attitude and whistle a merry tune for five thousand dollars.

Maybe.

A hard, quick tapping came at the driver's side window. Oliver jumped and shrieked, not in a manly fashion, feeling his heart jam into his throat as he turned and saw a silhouette at the window. His pulse calmed a little when he found it was Diane, Sabrina's older sister, leaning over and peeking in at him.

"Hey, stranger," she said as he rolled down the window to talk to her. "You waiting on Micah?"

"Yeah. Hey, let me get out of this thing. Stuffy in here."

Great. Diane. Not someone he was hoping to meet here. He grabbed his phone and ducked out of the car, locking up and following her to the sidewalk outside the dojo. She leaned against the glass, smirking as she watched the mini martial artists inside. Taller and leaner than her sister, Diane also had way more hair. Sabrina tended to keep hers shaved or incredibly short, and she had piercings where Diane kept a neutral, almost preppy look. Diane was pretty, smart . . . Exactly Micah's type.

"Haven't seen you in a while," Diane said, sipping from a half-empty diet soda.

"Been busy. Shop gets crazy this time of year. Dad gets me to take just about every shift I can," he replied. "Aren't you taking classes up at City Park?"

"Culinary stuff, uh-huh." She pulled her attention away from the kids. "Sabrina says you got into the school you wanted. That's big. Congrats."

"Hey, thanks." He grinned. "You know, it's nice to hear that. Haven't gotten to tell my old man yet. He was a wreck when I was filling out applications. I only got him to calm down because I said the whole thing was a long shot. Not sure he believed me."

"Ugh. I hear that. It's always the same with that family business bullcrap," Diane said with a roll of the eyes. "Mom woulda never gotten out of Baton Rouge if Granny hadn't died. Family business? More like family cult."

Oliver nodded, feeling a little less like a tense mess with each chuckle. "Amen."

"Just see you don't go takin' my sister off to Texas with you. I like her where she is."

"No, ma'am, wouldn't take her anywhere, not unless she wanted to come along."

Diane shook her head, reaching over to slug him playfully in the shoulder. "Who would keep me honest if she went off with you?"

"I thought you and Micah were, you know . . ." Oliver cleared his throat. Lord, but this was not his favorite subject. He didn't want to police his friend, even if Sabrina was asking him to do it. "Maybe he could look out for you."

"Yeah, 'cause we all know that boy's just full of good choices." She smirked and reached toward him again, but this time she just put her hand lightly on his arm. "I know Sabrina's been giving you shit about this whole thing. Don't you worry. I know who Micah is. I know what I'm getting myself into. It's just for fun, anyway. He'll go off to college, too, and then you won't have to worry about me getting mixed up with his crazy ass."

Well, that at least was a relief.

"Who are you calling crazy, woman?"

Micah roared toward them from the door, pouncing on them

both, pulling them in close for a hug with each arm.

"Man, you stink," Oliver muttered, wrestling out of his friend's grip.

"Didn't have time to shower, all right? Saw you two dawdling outside and thought it might be polite to hurry myself along." He stuck out his tongue, still holding Diane with one arm. "And what are you doing here? Did I miss a text or somethin'?"

Micah's gaze sharpened, the hard set of his jaw asking the silent question. *Did something go wrong with the drop-off?*

"Just bored is all," Oliver said with a shrug, shaking his head just the littlest bit for Micah's benefit. *No, everything went fine.*

"Ha. Don't let Sabrina hear you say that. She's spittin' mad that you haven't taken her out to celebrate your university thing."

"I know. I need to call her, but do you think I could borrow Micah for a sec? Just something I need to run by him real quick."

Just a little thing called five thousand dollars.

"Sure, but see you don't keep him too long, we had plans tonight."

"Plans. Yeah. It won't take but a moment." With that, Oliver tugged Micah aside, his arm damp with sweat through his shirt. They paused outside the auto parts store and the manager inside watched them while he closed up for the day, probably worried they were two no-good kids come to rob him.

Don't you worry, sir, we only rob the dead.

Ugh.

"What is it? You look like you been running all over hell's half acre." His gray eyes darkened and he glanced quickly toward Diane. "Everything okay with the, ya know, with our friend?"

"No, Micah, everything is *not fine*." How could he be so non-chalant about this? Oliver ran both hands over his greasy hair, puffing out a sigh. "Look, man, she wants us to keep going with this and now she's offering more money. A lot more money. So much money that I'm afraid I can't turn it down."

His friend went silent, rubbing his palm slowly over his goatee, staring at Oliver all the while. "Huh. Uh-huh."

"Is that all you have to say about this? I just don't get a good feeling about any of this. What are those creeps even doing? What are they using those bones for?" It came out like "using those bones fah" and it made him sound exactly like his father, with his deeper, occasionally impenetrable Southern drawl. Sabrina was always teasing him about it. She said it sounded cute, but to him it sounded trashy. Low. He was getting away from the family business, from the thing that had kept generations of his family trapped and going nowhere before. And thinking about his father just made him think of that damn text message waiting for him and for the *conversation* waiting for him, and how had this day gotten completely away from him to spin out of control?

Five thousand dollars. Nothing would be easy for that kind of cash, and here Micah looked like he was actually considering it.

"We can't say yes," Oliver said before his friend could respond. "We just can't."

"How much?"

He didn't want to say it. "Five thousand," he muttered.

"Five *grand*? Are you shittin' me?" Micah reeled back, rubbing his goatee faster now, his eyes all at once much brighter. Dancing.

"Say no, Micah. We have to say no."

"You're not interested in this? Not even a little bit?" He looked toward Diane, giddy almost, shaking his hands out like they had fallen asleep. "Five thousand is a lot. . . ."

"I know it is." Oliver turned away and took a fistful of his own hair, tugging. Maybe a little jolt of pain would set him to rights, put him back on the straight and reasonable path. "That shit we did is in the papers. Someone saw what we did. You have to say no," he whispered.

"Why me? Why do you keep saying that?"

His friend was right behind him then, breathing down his neck.

"Because if you say yes I'll feel like I should, too." Tired. So tired. He just wanted to sleep and wake up and for none of this to have happened. "Because I can't let you do it alone, ya know? And because, God, I *do* need the money. I do. Damn it all, I don't know what to do."

Micah's hand fell solemnly on his shoulder and stayed there. "Don't worry, man. I know what to do."

Chapter

10

*M*s. Marie Catherine Comtois lived in a white, ramshackle farmhouse set far back from the road on the route running between New Orleans and Baton Rouge. Heavy, lush falls of moss dripped off the trees crowding the front lawn, concealing the house itself behind a fragrant green curtain. White seeds like snowflakes drifted through the windless day, floating with eerie slowness through the doldrums of hot, damp air.

Oliver could practically taste the air, thick with honeysuckle from the garden that lined the front of the house and fanned out in a haphazard sprawl toward the overgrown, swampy forest encroaching on the property. It had obviously never been a great manor house, but at one time it was probably pretty and fresh, quaintly kept with green shutters on the windows and a turquoise blue door. Now the paint peeled off it like raw strips of sunburn, curling tight in the wet climate before scattering to join the tiny white seeds peppering the grass.

Weeds had taken over the walk up to the house, but Micah didn't seem to notice the disrepair. He certainly didn't apologize for it.

"Ms. Marie was like my aunt growing up," he explained, leading Oliver to the faded turquoise door and its brass knocker.

It was shaped like a mermaid. "If anyone in this damn world knows anything about these Bone Artist freaks, it would be her."

"Why's that?"

"Because she's about eight hundred years old, that's why." Micah chuckled, winking. "And don't let the old gal fool you. Back in the day she was a wild one. I've seen the pictures. Dance halls. Sailor boyfriends. The whole nine yards."

The trip felt like a waste of time to Oliver, who had already decided, firmly this time, that he was out. Briony had texted that morning, waking him out of a fog of heavy sleep to ask about the job. He had told her, in less than polite terms, to take her offer and shove it in a very specific place.

Micah had knocked, and now, gradually, the door was opening. His friend sprang into action, holding open the screen and swiftly relieving the tiny old woman of the weight of the door. Her skin looked like water-stained paper, dark spots dotting her hands and neck in thick clusters. But her eyes were sharp, bright and searching as she looked Oliver up and down.

"A'now who's this handsome young swain come to my door?" she asked, giggling like a teenager, even if it did sound a little croaky on the end.

"Ma'am, this is Oliver, Oliver Berkley. He's a good friend of mine."

"You said so on the phone," Ms. Marie said, reaching for the screen. Oliver grabbed it for her, joining them inside the house. It was stifling, a few overhead fans doing their level best to help but failing. Not even a fresh-baked pie could cover up the scent of decay and urine that drifted through the halls.

Still, it wasn't exactly dirty. The floors had been swept and

the shelves in reach were dusted. The old lady had gone to the trouble of doing her iron gray hair in big, retro curls, clipping one piece back with a pink barrette. That was probably her best dress, too, a white sundress with a daisy motif.

Oliver paused in the front hall, looking over the black-and-white photos of generations of family. The newest shots had been taken recently, hanging in a modern frame. Micah was in that one, standing with Ms. Marie and two women in their thirties, both with Marie's wide, brown eyes. The older photos were cluttered with many more people, all of them glaring out at Oliver with that strange, vacant quality folks seemed to have in the past, as if the bad technology rendered them utterly lifeless.

A few bunches of dried herbs hung above the pictures and a shelf with porcelain figures of Jesus, Mary, and a pair of hands clasped in a prayer pose. A cracked wooden placard swung from the front door behind him.

BLESS THIS HOUSE. PROTECT THIS HOUSE.

Trembling, shuffling, she brought them from the foyer to the sunroom on the left, motioning for them both to sit down. Cups of coffee and a cookie tray had been set out, and when Oliver went to sit down he found his cup lukewarm. She had probably set it out a half hour ago, fixing it whenever she had the energy.

"You live here on your own?" Oliver asked, trying to make conversation.

"Yes and no. My niece comes by every once in a while. Checks in on me and the like. Makes sure I ain't fallen over in a flower bed to lie with the petunias." She laughed at that and so did

Micah. Oliver joined in, coaxed by her infectious smile. Marie settled into an overstuffed chair, leaving the two boys to wedge themselves together onto an ancient loveseat that would have comfortably fit one moderately sized girl.

Oliver cradled the little saucer with his cookies in hands that felt clumsy and gigantic.

Micah didn't seem to notice the tiny china or the weird smells, perfectly at ease as he caught up with all the neighborhood gossip. A neighborhood that extended for some miles, Oliver guessed.

"Now I know this ain't a social call. Nobody brings theyselves out this far just to eat cookies." Marie narrowed her milky-brown eyes at Micah, tipping her head to the side. "You bein' good these days? You best not be in trouble or I'll get Sy down the street to hide you raw."

"That's just what I came to ask you about, ma'am," Micah said, dusting his powder-sugared fingers off on his jeans. "Me and Oliver here been doing a little work for some folks down t'New Orleans," he explained, his accent thickening by the minute, as if by passing through the door they had entered another segment of the state altogether.

"What kind of folks?" she drawled, studying them.

Oliver couldn't help but shrink away from her shrewd staring.

But Micah kept his tone light, cheerful even. "Some knuckleheads calling themselves the Bone Artists. Frauds, probably. Just nonsense, but Oliver got nervous so I thought it a good idea to check. . . ."

He rambled on, but Ms. Marie was obviously no longer listening, but was recoiling, pressing herself tightly against the back of the chair. "Your family raised you better than this, boy."

"So . . . they're not good, then," Oliver prompted. They weren't, of course, he knew that, but judging by her reaction it was worse than he'd anticipated. *What tipped you off, genius, the grave robbing or the creepy hideouts?*

Marie flicked her gaze between the two of them, shaking her head over and over again. He couldn't tell if she was shivering or just swiveling her head back and forth, back and forth. . . . "Back when I was a girl you didn't say those words. You didn't speak that name. You speak that name you get all that's evil in t'world coming to you."

"Whatever they do with these bones—" Micah began.

She was swift to cut him off, lifting a hand as if she could stopper his lips herself. "I won't repeat it. I won't say it, I won't. These folk—these are evil folk. The Bone Artists, they steal, and then they leave—body snatchers. Body *thieves*. They take your bones for black magics. *Witchcraft*. Satan's friend, that prince of they's is, He curse you and you're never right in the spirit again." Her voice rose and then fell to a sudden hush. She shook her head one last time, frowning, on the edge of tears as she looked at them as though they had both been taken far, far away.

"You won't never be right in the spirit again."

"She's a little on the religious side, if you couldn't tell," Micah had said, dropping Oliver back at the shop that afternoon. He had leaned over toward the passenger seat and the rolled-down window, gesturing at where Oliver stood on the sidewalk. "I wouldn't take everything she says seriously, all right? We're not talking a pinch of salt, here, we're talking the whole shaker. I mean, come on . . . Princes? Satan? I might believe in some dark stuff but let's not go crazy."

"I'm sure you're right," Oliver said, conjuring a thin smile. "But all the same . . ."

"No, you're right. Let's cut and run while we're ahead." Micah gave him a salute and a wink, leaning back into the steering wheel. "You seeing Sabrina tonight?"

"Maybe. It's getting on to supper. You seeing Diane?" Over his shoulder, Oliver heard the distinctive sounds of a séance going on inside. He hated séance night at the shop but it always brought out a bunch of tourists.

"Do you really have to ask?" He laughed, waggling his eyebrows. "Catch you later, man, we still need to do that big celebration. Don't keep stalling!"

"I'm not, I swear, just giving y'all time to plan the parade."

Micah snorted and honked the horn on his old Chrysler, pulling away from the curb and into the empty street.

The voices inside the shop swelled to meet him, but he dodged the door, aiming instead for the family apartment. His pocket buzzed and he slipped out his phone, wincing as he read the display.

The Dragon Lady.

She had her answer, what more could she want from him?

"Your answer is no? Is that your final decision?" it read.

Oliver texted back furiously, lips pursed with aggravation. There was no doubt in his mind that he needed out. Now. She was poison and he refused to go back for another dose.

The answer is and always will be: no. Leave me alone.

He was just a few steps from their front door when her reply came, fast enough that Oliver hadn't gotten his phone all the way inside his pocket. Just one word, and for some reason it chilled him more than her gaze or her sneer ever could.

Pity.

Chapter

11

*H*e jerked awake to Bon Jovi blaring into his pillow. Oliver flailed, grateful, for once, to be yanked out of his sleep. Out of dreams. A tall, dark shape had been watching him in his dreams, looming in the corner of his room, resolving into a human man but just the shadow of one. It watched him, it waited, getting closer to the bed whenever Oliver closed his eyes and opened them again.

But now he was awake and the only long shadow in the room came from the coat stand in the corner.

SHOT THROUGH THE HEART

It was Micah's ringtone. He scrambled for the phone with clumsy fingers, rubbing at his eyes, not believing them at first when he noticed the LED clock next to his bed read 3:26.

AND YOU'RE TO BLAME

He answered with a sigh, reasonably certain this was a butt dial and he'd just hear gross make-out noises on the other end. But no, it was his friend all right, and breathing hard into the receiver, so hard it distorted the sound, painfully loud to Oliver's half-asleep ear.

His friend's voice was frantic on the other end of the line. Oliver had only heard him that upset one other time, when they had climbed a nasty old chain-link fence in Bywater and Micah had sliced his palm open on a jagged link at the top. The cut clearly needed stitches—there had been blood soaking Micah's clothes, all down the front of his new Saints T-shirt. The blood was on Oliver, too, but somehow he remained calm, got Micah to pedal on his bike back through the neighborhood toward home. Then came Micah's grandmother and a trip to the hospital, and it was all fixed.

Oliver wasn't so sure any phone call or hospital could fix this. He could hear something sizzling and popping in the background, and his friend could barely breathe as he wheezed into the cell phone.

"Ollie? Ollie, oh shit, I'm so sorry," he said. "I'm sorry, I'm so, so sorry. . . ."

"Sorry? What do you mean? Slow down, man, what happened? Are you okay?"

Tears. Actual tears. This was the first time Micah had cried, no, not just cried, *sobbed*. There were sirens in the distance, growing louder over the sound of his friend's heaving, slobbery sobs into the phone.

"Calm down, okay? Calm down and tell me what happened. Do you need me to do something? Is there . . . Shit, Micah, just tell me how I can help!"

A long, shuddering breath. Another sob. A longer breath. The sirens were bearing down on him now, Oliver could tell, and that would mean soon Micah would have to go and deal with the police or the ambulance or whatever the hell that was.

"It's Diane," he whispered. "She's going to be okay, I think . . . I think . . . I hope . . . Oh, God, oh Jesus, please Oliver, please! The other driver—I don't know. I don't know if they're okay. If they're here. I can't *see* anything. The hospital. I need a hospital."

The line went dead.

"What!?" Oliver shrieked, slapping his own forehead. "No . . . no, no, no! Micah, you shithead. You ass! You can't just hang up, you can't do that."

He called back. No response. He called again. Nothing. Then he called Sabrina, shaking, knowing he would not like at all what he heard on the other end. But when she picked up there was a long, shuffling beat, the sound of bedsheets sliding around.

"Mmfffgh . . . He-hello?"

"Babe? Babe! Wake up. You have to get up now." He could hear his voice going high and hoarse. Panicked. What the hell was he supposed to do? "There's been an accident," he said, stumbling out of bed and searching the dark for his jeans. "I'm coming to pick you up."

In the end, Oliver was too nervous to drive. His father woke up from the commotion, wrenching the keys out of Oliver's hands and forcing him to wait while he got decent enough to drive to Sabrina's and then the hospital.

Oliver huddled in the passenger seat, on the phone with Sabrina until they reached her house, and then he joined her in the back, listening to Nick Berkley calmly call hospitals until he found Micah's location.

It was a blur. A haze. The only constant was the steady sound of his dad's soothing voice and Sabrina's clammy hand curled up in his. He watched the back of his dad's head as they jogged through the hospital halls, searching, searching. . . . How could his dad be this collected? Would he ever get that way? Did adults just wake up one day with that skill to keep a level head when everything else was going to hell?

He hated the stark, white neon of the hospital and the sickly smell. He wanted to laugh, thinking of Micah clutching his hand when he had to get stitches, both of them telling jokes to try to keep Micah from freaking out at the sight of so much blood.

There were no jokes this time.

They found Micah in an empty waiting room, oddly calm as a whirlwind of activity went on down the hall in surgery. The doors were closed and nobody was let in, but from the way Micah stared intently, too intently, at the corridor, Oliver knew that something bad had happened. Sabrina broke away, racing to Micah's side, grabbing him by the shoulders and shaking.

"Where is she?" she hissed, searching his face. "Where's Dee?"

"I couldn't do anything," Micah murmured, his eyes hollow. A bandage was taped across his forehead, big enough to conceal a large gash. Bruises had already begun forming along his cheekbones. The faint smell of whiskey hung around Micah, growing stronger whenever he gave another deep breath. "The driver . . . They came out of nowhere. I couldn't stop. I wasn't even going that fast, he just . . . He just came out of nowhere."

"Where. Is. She."

Sabrina slapped him, not hard, but enough to make both Oliver and his dad reach for her, coaxing her away from Micah. But the blow stirred something in him. Light danced back into his eyes, focusing quickly and pinpointing on Sabrina.

"She's hurt," Micah murmured, scrunching up his face. It

looked like he was going to cry again any second. "She's hurt real bad."

Real bad was obviously not the whole story. They got it out of him in bits and pieces, nurses running back and forth behind them in the background. Oliver didn't want to think about what that meant. Micah's face was ashen. He had seen something, something terrible.

And the alcohol on his breath . . . Oliver glanced toward the hall leading back toward the elevators, convinced the police would be showing up any second to question Micah.

The story came together slowly. They were driving back to Diane's house, maybe a little faster than normal. They had broken curfew, and Micah was worried about upsetting her family. Diane didn't care, she was having a good time. They were crossing the Causeway into the city and the driver came out of nowhere, gaining on him and then swerving, slamming into the driver's side door before Micah could react. The car veered and hit the right-side safety rail. They skidded and skidded but didn't go over into the water. A miracle, that. By the time the car stopped, Micah could hardly move. Airbag in his face. Car horns. Rubberneckers slowing down to see what had happened. To help. He was too dazed to get the car's license plate. To even remember a color.

And the worst part was, Diane was just silent. She had screamed, once, on impact, and then nothing.

At that, Sabrina dropped to the floor. Oliver knew what she was thinking because he was thinking it, too. He scooped her into his arms, holding her, letting her hot, constant tears wet the shoulder of his T-shirt. The linoleum bit into his tailbone but he let it go, just holding. Just sitting.

Then Sabrina's family began to arrive and one by one they started to guide her away, question her, and one by one they began to look at Micah like he was a cockroach. Like it was all his fault.

Oliver stood next to his father and next to Micah, none of them speaking. Sometimes Nick would pipe up to fill the air or offer to grab everyone coffee. It felt like nobody was speaking English, like nobody was making sense. Where did you put your feet when the Earth wouldn't stop spinning? What did you say when a girl was dying down the hall?

A nurse had come into the waiting room. Sabrina and her family swarmed, understandably, and Oliver went to join them, pausing when his phone buzzed in his pocket. He'd forgotten all about it. He was so dazed he didn't even question who would be calling at that hour, and he didn't bother to study the display before accepting the text and staring down at it.

He couldn't hear what the nurse was saying. He didn't want to, didn't need to.

"My condolences," it read, "—Briony."

Down the hall, the elevator doors dinged. It took Oliver a moment to focus his eyes, dazed. Just like he thought—the officers were here, two of them, striding toward their huddled group, eyes grimly determined and fixed on Micah.

Chapter 12

*S*leep was a distant fantasy. Oliver couldn't imagine dropping into bed anyway, simultaneously wired and exhausted. There was no turning his brain off, not now, not when he was spending the rest of this miserable night at a police station.

He tore himself away from Sabrina and her family to ride with his dad over to the police station. The front of the building loomed high and pointed, the red brick facade reminding Oliver of an old schoolhouse. Traffic in and out at that hour was brisk, but the civilians being hauled in and out looked to be in varying states of drunkenness, some being taken out of the drunk tank, others going in.

Micah among them.

No, it was worse than that. He wasn't falling over himself or slurring his words, but he was just tipsy or tired enough to belong nowhere near a moving vehicle. And he had been in one and Diane had been with him. *Idiot.*

"You said it," Oliver's father said.

He had said that last thing aloud then.

Oliver shook his head, slumped over, shuffling into the station with his dad, knowing Micah was somewhere inside. "Maybe I should have stayed at the hospital."

"Sabrina has family, Micah doesn't."

"Yeah, even so . . . I don't know if he deserves us right now."

"Your friends don't stop being your friends the second they screw up."

Oliver nodded. "Sure. He said it was someone else, someone trying to run them off the road." He thought of the text from Briony and shivered. Inside, the police station was freezing cold, the noisy AC unit jacked up to combat the humidity outside. "But I guess he would say that, given . . . Idiot."

"Ollie—"

"No, Dad, this isn't the first time he's been a screw-up. Trust me on that one."

A rumpled, coffee-stained officer directed them to the waiting area. He shrugged in response to their questions about Micah. No, he couldn't say when he would be out. No, they couldn't see him. Yes, a lawyer had been contacted for him. Yes, they were free to wait.

Oliver paced, his dad watching him march back and forth under the harsh lights.

"You have every right to be mad, what he did—"

"It's not just this. It's . . ." The lying, the grave robbing, and now *this*. "Diane is dead, Dad."

"I know."

"Because of *him*."

"I know that, too."

"And he might have been drunk. Jesus!" Oliver put the *might* in there for Micah's sake. Maybe they had been drinking earlier in the night and he'd spilled on himself. There could have been a bottle in the car that shattered in the wreck. Any number of possibilities could be true, but the knot in Oliver's stomach told him none of them really were. He stopped pacing and turned to look at his father, chewing the inside of his cheek. "If someone is dead weight, how long do you hold on? What if they're dragging you down with them?"

Muffled voices down the hall cut short his father's response. Oliver twisted around, jogging past the water cooler and coffee dispenser to the reception desk. He spotted Micah's scruffy, dark head over the shoulder of a short, compact man in a trim suit. It was after five in the morning—how did anyone look that presentable at that hour?

Escorted by officers, Micah was smiling, chatting and chuckling with the guy in a suit, whose briefcase and smart spectacles broadcast *lawyer* loud and clear. Not just lawyer, but *pricey* lawyer. Oliver couldn't imagine where Micah had found the scratch to pay the retainer on someone like this.

"Ollie!" Micah perked up the second he saw him, his brows tenting over his glasses. "You didn't have to come here. I mean, I'm glad you did. It's good to have someone here."

The lawyer snorted softly at that. The officers pulled away, leaving them in the waiting room while Oliver's father hovered in the background.

"I thought you were smoked," Oliver said, relieved despite his misgivings. "But I knew you weren't drunk. That's not you. Sabrina's going to—I mean she's still pissed, yeah, but this wasn't your fault."

Micah pursed his lips, glancing at his sneakers. "Look, there's no pretty way to put this, man, but—"

"But my client is smart enough not to comment further," the

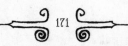

lawyer said tartly, narrowing his eyes at Micah. "Just like we discussed."

"Right. Just like we discussed." Micah shrugged as if to say, *what can you do?* and flashed Oliver a sheepish grin, scratching his whiskery chin. "You understand."

Understand? *Understand?*

Oliver flinched, opening and closing his mouth until the right words, or some of them, came to mind. "Hang on, are you saying you *were* drunk and you got in that car with Diane?"

"He's not saying anything," the lawyer replied, taking Micah in hand and jerking him toward the desk. "You need to be processed out, Micah, and this conversation is over."

"Micah—"

"It's going to turn out all right," Micah said, giving another sheepish smile, one that ended swiftly. The lawyer manhandled him away, but Micah glanced over his shoulder, watching Oliver as he slid away. "Tell Sabrina I'm sorry, okay? Tell her I'll . . . tell her I'll make it up to her somehow."

Chapter

13

Freedom!

It was the first text from Micah in months. Understandable, given that he had been locked up in juvenile detention for the whole of the summer. Oliver stared at his phone, numb, tapping his foot under the table. The lunch rush had come and gone at the sandwich shop, the din of voices, laughter, and chewing rising and then falling all while Oliver waited on his dad. He hadn't expected the text from Micah, but then none of his friend's time in juvie made much sense to him.

There'd been no trial. Micah had pled guilty and gone away, but Oliver could swear he ought to be serving a longer sentence. First offense. Good conduct. He could imagine the answers Micah would give before even asking the questions.

Staying with Grams in Shreveport. Catch up soon?

Oliver didn't respond. He didn't know how. Whatever fond memories existed of Micah's grandmother and her insanely delicious gumbo were now tainted. Sabrina was in therapy twice weekly, and Oliver had begun to wonder if maybe he should be going with her.

He flicked Micah's message away, checking instead for word

from his father. His knee bounced faster as he scanned the deli, the counter, the chairs, the back entrance, and then the sidewalk outside. An hour late was nothing for his dad, but he had only texted once to mention the delay.

"I get it," Oliver muttered, fussing with his hair and running his tongue nervously over the scar on his lip. "Punishment. Real mature, dad."

His father wasn't at all fond of the idea of Oliver leaving for UT Austin, and that was just one more tally in the SUCK column for the summer. As soon as Oliver had broken the news, his dad had grown distant, cutting back Oliver's hours at the store more and more, either to prepare for the upcoming separation or to make things harder on Ollie. Oliver had gotten the hint, picking up a few jobs on the side fixing friends' cars, clinging desperately and guiltily to the cash he had made from helping Briony.

Sometimes the urge to pick up the phone and text her, asking for work, broke his will to never, ever walk the seedy path again. But each time he almost crumbled, he remembered that text after the car wreck.

Briony was involved somehow. How else would she have known so soon? Micah might have been drunk and stupid, but Oliver absolutely believed that someone else was involved.

The waitress took another slow pass by his table, rolling her eyes when Oliver said he was still fine with ice water. He had long ago finished the brownie he'd bought to nibble on while he waited for his dad. But it was growing obvious that his father was a no-show. One last lunch together in August before school started, was that so much to ask?

It was. It definitely was when you were leaving the family

business—and New Orleans—behind.

His phone jumped in his hands, and Oliver clasped it harder, fumbling before bringing it to his ear, his dad's smiling face appearing on the display as the ring chimed.

"You standing me up?" Oliver laughed, trying to lighten the very real accusation. "Not cool, man."

Static spiked on the other end and Oliver jerked his head away. The crackling died down, an incoherent voice rumbling through the static.

"Your reception blows. Are you in the car or going under a bridge or something?"

". . ."

"Dad? Hello? Call me back in a sec, see if that helps—"

". . . the bridge . . ."

His voice was just a scrape, just a whisper. Oliver could hear the pain in it. "Dad? Are you okay? Where are you?"

"I saw them. . . ." A wheezing breath. "I saw them follow me."

The line went dead after a few seconds of breathing and then silence. Oliver shoved the table away from him and ignored the looks he got, dashing for the door, trying his dad's number again. No answer. He tried again, swearing, tumbling out of the shop and into the thick, wet humidity of August. Clouds sat low and dark over the city, clustered, the utter stillness of the air foretelling the rain to come.

A siren began in the distance, somewhere to Oliver's left as he tried his dad's line again. This time someone picked up and then immediately ended the call. The siren screamed louder as it neared, cars gradually slowing and parting as one, then two, then three police cruisers sped by. Oliver sprinted to his car, palms slick with icy sweat as he struggled to back out and navigate the street choked with idling cars.

He leaned on the horn, setting his jaw, heedless of the windows rolling down so drivers could scream at him as he weaved recklessly ahead. The bridge. If his dad was returning from an antiques delivery out of the city then Oliver could bet which route he would take on the return trip. The speeding police cars carved a path through traffic, and Oliver followed as closely as he could, flying through stilled four-way stops and traffic lights. There was nothing ahead of him but his father, somewhere, murmuring with that soft, pained voice.

Their last lunch before Oliver went off to school, one cordial afternoon between father and son, was that too much to ask of the universe?

He lost track of the minutes, driving with one hand and dialing his father repeatedly with the other, leaning hard toward the steering wheel as the threatening clouds above opened up, rain driving at the windshield. Buildings and neighborhood blocks gave way to nothingness; the unobscured, open view of the Causeway unfolded under the black clouds. He was close.

The bridge. I saw them follow me.

Chapter
14

*O*liver drove as far as he could, stopped within half a mile of turning onto the Causeway. A blockade went up as he watched, disobeying the police officer who stood in the downpour, directing with his hands for cars to turn around. Another set of police cars began the process of shutting down the traffic trying to flow toward the Causeway, preventing anyone from even approaching that lane of the bridge.

His breath had caught long before he turned off the ignition. Beyond the blockade he could make out the remains of a shitty old white pickup truck. It had been pancaked into the side of the Causeway, one tire teetering precariously over the edge, a gentle nudge from dropping into the lake.

Oliver parked wherever, leaving the door to his car open as he drifted out of it, wiping the rain from his eyes only as a formality, only because he needed to see. Flares cracked to life on the road, neon red fires kindling on the pavement, doing nothing to cut through the raincloud darkness. The officer directing traffic didn't see him as he approached the yellow tape. Oliver ducked under, sneakers colliding with debris and crystalline chunks of glass that sparkled, reflecting the red flare light.

His mind tricked him into thinking it was a different white pickup truck. Of course it was. Nothing was for sure until it

was for sure. Nothing could convince him it was his dad's truck until there was absolute proof. This was a coincidence until it was a tragedy. But he still couldn't breathe. His pulse knew what his mind refused to accept.

"Whoa, hey kid, you have to get back in your vehicle and turn around." An officer intercepted him, a tall, thin woman with cowlike, sympathetic eyes and yellow hair. She ducked and took a closer look at him. "Hey? Sir? Can you hear me? Did you hear what I said?"

"My dad," Oliver murmured, staring past her. "That's . . . that's my dad's truck."

"What? Are you sure about that?" She glanced around, at the truck and then at the ambulance and fire truck parked horizontally across the lane. "I need to see some ID, kid."

Oliver pulled his wallet out of his jeans and handed her the whole thing. He handed her his keys. He didn't trust his hands to hold anything anyway. Her grip on him loosened and Oliver continued forward, as if he had no control over his own momentum, as if the twisted-up truck had caught him in a tractor beam. Something caught on his shoe and stuck, gluey. Oliver wiggled his leg but it wouldn't come off. He stopped, watching as three drenched firemen cut away and wrenched off the truck's folded-up door.

What was it they called that thing? The Jaws of Life?

A pale, limp hand slid into view, curled up on what was left of the passenger's side seat. The flares crackled. The sirens all around him flickered and flickered, dyeing that single hand blue and then red. The officer behind him barked into her radio, asking for help, more help, more assistance, for Christ's sake the guy's kid had shown up, could she get some damn help already?

Someone grabbed him by the arm and yanked him back. That same officer.

"It's my dad," Oliver said, tugging against her. "It's my dad!" He panicked, but she was strong, holding him, and soon two more officers jogged over to help her, restraining him as the EMTs hurried in after the firemen, a stretcher folded out and waiting behind them.

He didn't know what he was screaming anymore, just that he was screaming. He didn't know what he was seeing, only that his father was being taken away in pieces.

They carried him away. Forced him away. Wet through and freezing, Oliver couldn't feel any of it. His throat felt raw, and when they sat him down in the back of an open ambulance, a dry, brown blanket draped over his shoulders, he couldn't even grasp the edges of the fabric with his trembling fingers.

"How did you know to come here?" an officer was asking, gently. They were all perfectly nice to him now that he had stopped shrieking.

Oliver didn't answer. What did it matter? He couldn't save his dad, and the reasons why seemed pointless to consider. He shifted, his sneaker scraping the pavement. That damn gluey bullshit was still stuck to his foot. Suddenly it was the only thing worthy of his attention. How dare it. How dare it annoy him right then? How dare anyone touch him or look at him or ask him anything at all?

He bent down and blindly groped at the bottom of his shoe, tearing away the plasticky strip with a ferocious tear of his fist.

He almost tossed it away, but the dark green color snagged on a memory. Unrolling the wad of torn plastic, Oliver stared down at the sticker. A bumper sticker.

He couldn't breathe again, and the cold and the rain and the officer touching his shoulder felt a million miles away.

PROUD PARENT OF AN HONOR ROLL STUDENT

His phone buzzed in his pocket, the one item he hadn't handed over to the police for safekeeping. The officer sighed and wandered away, giving up on Oliver and his dazed silence. When she was gone, Oliver retrieved his phone, realizing he should call Sabrina, call Micah, call anyone at all who could make sense of this for him.

He had deleted her number, but he recognized the odd area code. Briony.

Come back to work for us, Oliver. Your debt is not repaid.

PROUD PARENT OF AN
HONOR ROLL STUDENT

Chapter

15

*S*abrina had fallen asleep hours ago. For her sake, Oliver let her think he had done the same. Small comforts, she'd said. That was what had helped her after Diane died. A warm mug of tea. A hot shower. A familiar bed. Home. Friends. He had let her do all those things for him, culminating in the two of them cuddled up watching *The Princess Bride* on repeat until they both fell asleep.

Well, *she* fell asleep. Oliver stared at the muted film, the actors mouthing lines he knew by heart.

You killed my father. Prepare to die.

At least the tears had stopped. Oliver hadn't realized a person could just keep crying and crying with no sound or anything else coming out, just relentless tears that triggered at the smallest, stupidest thing. They almost triggered again when he picked his half-dead phone up and shrugged out of the blanket covering him and Sabrina. She snored lightly while he dialed Micah again. His entire call log for the past three hours was filled with that one number.

Where the hell was that kid? Why now, of all times, did he decide to disappear? Micah had ditched out on the Bone Artists and Briony just as much as Oliver had, and now Oliver believed with every sinew in his body that his friend had been run off the road intentionally, just like his dad.

He almost yelped in shock when the other end livened up and Micah's face greeted him groggily.

"Micah? Jesus Christ, dude, I've been trying to get in touch with you all night!"

"What? What is . . . Is everything all right?" He sounded more awake at least.

"It's my dad." That was it. That was all he could manage. The tears started again and Oliver smothered them in the neck of his tee, trying not to wake Sabrina. "His truck. The Causeway. It's just like . . . just like you said it happened to you."

Micah breathed heavily on the other end. "Can we meet somewhere to talk about this, man?"

"What? *No.* No, it's . . . I can't think about driving anywhere. I'm with Sabrina." He squeezed his eyes shut, pulling off the blankets, suddenly much too warm. Pinpricks crawled over his forearms. "I got a message from Briony," he hissed. "More than one. One after your accident and one tonight. It's not a coincidence, Micah. They're watching me. They're watching *us.*"

His friend gave a cold bark of laughter. "That's insane, Ollie. That's . . . That all ended months ago."

"Maybe for you," Oliver muttered. "She's not texting you? She's not threatening you?"

"I don't know what to tell you, man."

"That's *bullshit.*" He winced, lowering his voice again. "That's not an answer. My dad is dead. Diane is dead. What the fuck is wrong with you?"

"Me? Nothing is wrong with me. Shit. I'm waking up Grams with this. I'll be in touch tomorrow."

"Micah, wait—"

"I said I'll be in touch."

Oliver stayed with the phone stuck to his ear for a moment, stunned. He had never heard that voice come out of his friend. Vicious. Detached. It cut. Oliver lowered the phone, dragging his eyes from Sabrina's huddled silhouette to the open and half-packed duffel bags in the corner. In the morning he would unpack them. He couldn't leave now, and maybe he couldn't leave ever.

Chapter

16

Ollie—

I know it's been a few days since I said I'd be in touch. Okay, scratch that, a few weeks, but I needed time. I think you did, too. But I've been thinking about you and your dad, and I wanted to tell you how sorry I am and that I know what you must be going through. It sucks to feel alone. It sucks even worse to think you're alone because of something you did or didn't do.

I'm not emailing to tell you how to live your life, but it helped me to go forward. Juvie was shit at first, then I realized it could be fine. It could be whatever I wanted it to be. So I kept my head down and I worked hard and that got me friends where it counted. Good behavior. That's all it takes—in life, in work, in juvie, in whatever.

I heard through the grapevine that you're not going to Austin. That's a mistake, Ollie. You have to move forward. It's the only thing that helped me. Look, I'm moving forward, okay? Part of that means coming to grips with the truth. The truth is, I was drunk and irresponsible that night with Diane and she died because of it. That's my burden, and I accept it. I don't know how your dad got into that collision, but it was an accident and that's what killed him. Mistakes happen. Accidents happen. You have to let all this conspiracy shit go. Sometimes it's hard to just accept that the world isn't fair, that it's a screwed-up place.

But it can be a good place, too. Hell, I'm going to college. Me! Can you believe it? A decent one, too. The dean at this fancy-pants New Hampshire college reached out, heard some nice things about me from an old boss. See? Good things can and will fall in your lap, Ollie. I can help them fall in your lap if you want me to, but I know you're probably still sore and that's fine.

Think about what I said, okay? I miss you, man.

You take care of yourself, Oliver.

Micah

THE
WARDEN

The last temptation is the greatest treason:
to do the right deed for the wrong reason.

—T. S. ELIOT, *MURDER IN THE CATHEDRAL*

You know how I define "idealism"? Youth's final luxury.

—DOUG WRIGHT, *QUILLS*

PROLOGUE

This exasperating girl still exhibits a strong tendency toward selflessness. Her naive obsession with fruitless do-goodery could prove hindrance or help—I need only convince her that by embracing my vision, she will, in fact, be doing good. My observation of her continues, particularly where the Catalyst is concerned. I thought her compassion for his condition troublesome at first, but no, I will use their deepening connection to my advantage.

—Excerpt from Warden Crawford's journals—June

CHAPTER
№ 1

Brookline Hospital, Spring 1968

*I*t was raining. Pouring, actually—a fact that Madge, Jocelyn's bus companion for the last six hours, delighted in reiterating every other minute.

"Do you know how long it takes to get my curlers to cooperate?" Madge sighed, standing next to Jocelyn on the dark pavement, a copy of *Photoplay* held over her head to ward off the raindrops. The magazine buckled in the middle, sluicing water down the front of Madge's coat. "So much for making a good impression," she muttered.

Jocelyn smirked, warm and dry under the ugly but decidedly practical plastic rain bonnet. "It looks like you've got a condom on your head, dummy," Madge had teased on the bus, scrunching up her nose behind her *Photoplay*, so that both she and the full-color image of Jackie Kennedy were giving Jocelyn less-than-impressed looks.

"Now who's the dummy?" Jocelyn said as they turned to walk up the drive. They stepped through the lingering exhaust cloud the bus had left behind as a final, indifferent good-bye. The driver had glanced at them repeatedly during the trip. Jocelyn hadn't noticed it at first, and then maybe she'd thought he was

just admiring Madge. Madge *was* incredibly admirable.

A few grumbles from Madge later and they were clicking their way across the paving stones toward the hospital. It looked . . . well, less cheery than it had in the hiring brochures pushed on them at their recruitment meetings. Jocelyn and Madge had graduated together from Grace Point in Chicago with Bachelors of Science in Nursing, Jocelyn with honors, Madge with style.

In the brochure, Brookline shone like a lighthouse on a rock, white, pristine, all glimmering windows and tidy lawns. Patients beamed from their beds or wheelchairs. Nurses smiled with appropriate modesty and wisdom together in the halls. Doctors scrutinized charts, mustaches askew from the depths of their concentration.

"Goodness gracious," Madge mumbled, drawing to a halt at exactly the same point Jocelyn did.

"It's not so bad," Jocelyn insisted. She forced a smile, first at the hospital and then at Madge. "Cheer up, buttercup. We're hired. We're *professionals*."

"*Single* professionals," Madge said, giggling. "Oh gosh, am I blushing? I think I'm blushing. It's too good to be true." She cast a long look around, her smile wavering a little as another gush of rain poured down her front. Jackie Kennedy was looking severely worse for wear. "And here I so wanted to say: we're not in Kansas anymore. Or Chicago, I guess. You get the idea. But the rain's just the same."

"Are you kidding? We're practically New Yorkers," Jocelyn teased. A black wrought-iron fence surrounded the front grounds of the hospital. The building sat well back from the fencing, looming, a little hunched, either from the nearness of the dark clouds or from a shoddy foundation. To the left, New Hampshire College buildings encroached, but only a few students ran back and forth in the quadrangle, their heads bowed under umbrellas. Jocelyn turned back to the fence and stepped up to the gate, pushing on the handle and wincing at the rusty screech that followed. "Yup. Very cosmopolitan."

"Now who's the spoilsport? Come on, let's get inside. I'm drenched." Madge hurried beyond her, one hand desperately holding the magazine over her buttercup yellow hair, the other toting along her one and only bag. "What are you waiting for? I want to meet the staff. And the doctors! And my future husband!"

Jocelyn rolled her eyes, but she had to smile; Madge was right, this was a big day for them both. She hurried up the paving stones, her eyes flicking skyward at the suggestion of a silhouette in one of the windows above. It was there and then it was gone, but as Jocelyn ducked inside the hospital, she couldn't shake the feeling that she was being watched.

*W*arden Crawford looked up at her briefly in between each page of her application.

Jocelyn squirmed. Wasn't this already a done deal? She thought her application had been approved. Why else would she have made the exhausting trip from Illinois to the coast? That bumpy, cold bus trip hadn't exactly been a Tijuana pleasure cruise.

Keep still, she reminded herself. *Eyes forward.*

The warden's office was surprisingly cluttered for a doctor's. She always imagined men like him leading lives as clean and upright as a drill sergeant's. But papers stuck out of every desk drawer and cabinet, almost haphazardly. Her eye twitched. She was a neat person by nature, a character trait that her supervisor at school had said made her an excellent candidate for nursing. An eye for detail was absolutely required—nursing was hard, unforgiving work, with long hours and immense amounts of pressure and stress.

If a grill cook flips the burger too late the meat is burned, oh well, her supervisor used to say. *If you make a mistake a patient could die. Do you understand me, Ash? Are you going to flip the meat too late?*

Jocelyn bit the inside of her cheek. She hated that image. She hated that it made her think of humans, of human flesh, like meat.

"Chicago is a long way from here," Warden Crawford said lightly. He had a twinkle in his voice, like every statement might turn sharply into a joke. "I don't think our pizza measures up."

"Not a problem, sir," she responded crisply. "More of a chowder girl myself."

That drew a warm laugh from him. He sat back in his leather chair and put down her application, removing his spectacles and letting them settle in his white coat pocket. "A sense of humor. Good. You'll need that here. It can be morbid work, Ms. Ash. Sometimes you need to laugh or risk going mad yourself."

Jocelyn flinched. Right. Gallows humor. Madge had warned her that doctors could be crass, even rude. *It's just how they talk*, she'd said. *It's just how they blow off steam.* Anyway, Jocelyn couldn't protest; doctors were treated as gods. Nurses were expected to stand when they entered the room, like they were royalty or something. The whole thing seemed eye-rollingly over the top. Didn't anyone want to stand for the ladies changing bedpans day in and day out?

"You're young," he observed. Jocelyn flinched again. His lips hovered between a smile and a scowl. "Perhaps too young."

"My evaluations speak for themselves," she said. Her voice had become pinched, and so had a nerve in her neck that made her twitch with distress. No matter what, she was not getting back on a bus to Chicago.

Warden Crawford toyed with his spectacles for a moment, pulling them out of his pocket, unfolding the stems, and then putting them right back where they had been. "And what brought you to this profession?"

"I want to—"

"And don't say you want to help people." He chuckled, the twinkle back in his voice as she stammered into silence. "That's what everyone says."

"It's probably also true," Jocelyn replied, maybe impertinently. She never knew quite when to keep her mouth shut, and now she felt more words spill out faster than she could control. "I have to say, I'm confused, sir. My teachers at Grace Point told me there was a job here. Is that not the case?"

Warden Crawford jerked his head back, either in surprise or offense, she wasn't quite sure. He had a young face, but the gray at his temples suggested a more distinguished age. And he was handsome, exactly the kind of serious but gentle doctor Madge was no doubt hoping to snare. Her eyes strayed to his left hand. No ring. It seemed odd that a man of his age would be single. Jokes aside, Camford wasn't exactly a bustling metropolis. Surely there were plenty of women eager to snare a handsome doctor?

He shuffled her papers and then tucked them into one of his messy desk drawers. "Terrence in counseling is always warning me about hiring redheads. Too lippy, he says. Too feisty." Warden Crawford stood, laughing again, extending a hand to her across his desk. "We could use a little more fire around here. This isn't a place for the faint of heart, which makes me think you'll fit right in, Ms. Ash."

Phew. She had the job and she could breathe again and stop clutching her rain bonnet like a life jacket.

"Thank you, sir. Really, thank you. And, it's true, you know. I want to help people."

"Don't we all?" he murmured, a cold, intense light brightening his gaze. "Don't we all."

For the first time in her life, Jocelyn felt like she not only had a purpose but a clear-cut course, too. She saw little of the doctors for the first few weeks and even less of Warden Crawford. Assigned to simple, straightforward tasks, Jocelyn began to wear holes in her shoes from making frequent trips up and down the first and second level patient halls, changing sheets, delivering tiny paper cups of medicines, and swapping out, disinfecting, and returning bedpans. Gradually she began to recognize the faces underneath the little white paper hats—the other nurses were cordial, but none of them came close to her friendship with Madge.

Madge, who still managed to find time to flirt with orderlies and doctors alike; there was no telling how she did it. For her part, Jocelyn could barely scrabble together a spare minute to eat lunch.

But that was all right. She had expected hazing, but instead Nurse Kramer assigned her some of the calmer patients. In particular, Jocelyn liked Mrs. Small in 214—her dementia had progressed to a point where her stories varied day to day, but every once in a while the old woman described the fishing trips she used to take with her husband, and Jocelyn would listen intently, giving the patient a sponge bath or trying to coax her to eat breakfast. She would wonder where Mr. Small was now. Had he died before her or had he abandoned this gentle soul? Jocelyn had watched her own grandmother succumb to a similar disease, and she was the only family member who'd bothered

trying to talk to her in the hardest days of her illness. The days when her grandmother would forget who Jocelyn was, sometimes becoming so afraid that she grew violent.

It had pushed Jocelyn into nursing, that sense of injustice, that conviction that nobody, no matter how hurt or ill or old, deserved to deal with something like that alone.

Jocelyn checked the visitation schedule every morning and at the end of every shift, but nobody ever came to see Mrs. Small. It was disappointing every time, she thought tonight, closing up the bound schedule and giving a polite smile to a passing nurse. Mrs. Small could at least look forward to Jocelyn listening to her stories and laughing in all the right places.

By the time Jocelyn reached the dormitory level, Madge was already asleep in their room. Jocelyn mustered the energy to shrug out of her uniform, splash a little water on her face in the communal bathroom, brush her teeth, and shuffle back to their room. A stack of books sat unread next to her cot. As soon as her head touched the pillow, she was deeply, darkly asleep.

She thought the screams were in her nightmares until they grew so sharp and loud her head split open in pain.

The nursing dormitories lay between the floor for doctors above and the floor for miscellaneous staff and orderlies below. Sandwiched between them, Jocelyn's nights had until this point been restful. She flew up and out of bed as if jerked by a puppet master's strings. The screams came again, just as shrill and clear now that she was awake. She had counted herself lucky to be roomed with Madge, who snored only lightly and slept like the dead, her big, movie starlet eyes hidden behind a floral mask. Now she wished Madge were awake to consult.

The scream hadn't caused so much as a hitch in Madge's breathing.

But Jocelyn was awake now. Painfully awake. Her head throbbed, half from exhaustion and half from the shock of that noise knifing through her dreams. She pulled her cotton night-robe tighter over her pajamas, pressing bed-warmed feet to icy linoleum. A shiver traveled up through the floor, and she looked at the small blue clock on the bedside table. Two in the morning. For God's sake, she would need all the sleep she could get for another brutally busy day.

This isn't a place for the faint of heart.

"Ain't that the truth," she muttered, padding to the window. Even the staff rooms had bars on the windows, and tonight the bars obscured the heavy clouds and the downpour that had continued all day. The grounds below had become oversaturated and sludgy—once bright tulip beds turned into troughs of scattered blooms, flashes of color like the sad remnants of a parade.

At least there was moonlight to see by. Their room was small and sparsely furnished. Madge had already tacked a few magazine images to the wall over her bed, and whoever had lived there before had left a ceramic Minnie Mouse figurine on the windowsill. The paint had chipped, leaving Minnie looking like she had gone a few rounds with Sugar Ray Robinson. Jocelyn picked up the figurine, smirking at its lopsided grin. She wiped her thumb across Minnie's face and more of the cheap paint flecked off, sticking to her skin.

Another scream from the bowels of the hospital startled her, the figurine slipping out of her grasp. It hit the linoleum hard, cracking at the neck. Jocelyn bent to scoop it up, cradling the figurine gently, worried she might deepen the crack in the head that mirrored her own splitting headache.

"Damn," she whispered, standing and placing the figure on the bedside table.

With a sigh, Jocelyn pulled her robe shut again and went to Madge's side, trying to shake her friend awake. Madge groaned and pawed at her, then rolled over and continued to snore. Maybe it wasn't fair to deny her much-needed sleep. And anyway, this was a hospital for the mentally unstable, Jocelyn reminded herself. The patients could be suffering from any number of ailments. The worst kinds. The ones that couldn't be fixed with bandages or stitches or a quick dose of aspirin.

But it worried her that the scream sounded like a child's.

Jocelyn knew the lobby and patient floors inside and out now, but this screaming sounded like it was coming from far, far away. She paused at the door. There would be orderlies assigned to help the girl, surely. Nurses were probably even now there with her, trying their best to calm the little girl and get her back to sleep.

Still . . . Jocelyn couldn't imagine returning to bed. It didn't matter what Warden Crawford said, she wanted to help people. She *needed* to help people. Her mother kindly referred to it as a calling, but Jocelyn knew it for what it was—a compulsion.

She collected a sweater from the closet and pulled it over her pajamas, leaving her robe folded neatly over the footboard of her bed. Her shoes were just as cold as her feet, and she shook off another shiver as she carefully, quietly slipped out the door and into the dimly lit hallway beyond.

The corridors darkened as she descended through the hospital. Jocelyn hugged her sweater to her stomach, shuffling along with tiny steps. It was ridiculous for her to feel so scared. This was a hospital, not even that different from the familiar halls of her nursing program and before that her high school. Not that she'd stayed in either place for long. She had tested out of her studies early. Genius-level intelligence, her guidance counselor had said. Incredible aptitude. She'd wanted to be a doctor, but there were so few female doctors, it just seemed like a waste of time to pursue. A nurse was the next best thing, and maybe the status quo would change one day and she could go back to school, put that incredible aptitude to work. For now, that aptitude had catapulted her in short succession from school to nursing studies to here.

Brookline.

The lobby offered a brief respite from the cold and the dark. Warm, cheerful lamps glowed at all hours, illuminating the waiting area with its clean, blue chairs and straightened piles of magazines. The general reception desk was vacant at this hour, but a young, sandy-haired orderly dozed behind the medicine dispensary window, his chin cupped in his palm.

The screams from below apparently hadn't bothered him.

Was she hearing things? First Madge and now him . . . How could anyone sleep through the noise? Maybe she had dreamed the whole thing. No. She had an instinct for these things. Jocelyn tiptoed past the orderly, toward the basement levels, which she had never had a reason to venture anywhere near before.

Nobody had told her in detail what was housed down there. Supplies, most likely, the endless pills and bottles and towels that every hospital needed, and that appeared every day on the patient floors. A boiler room, perhaps? But whatever it was, she couldn't believe any patients would need to be kept so far from the main levels.

The screams had died down. Jocelyn tiptoed silently to Warden Crawford's office and paused. A light glowed from under the door. Two in the morning and he was still at work? That was dedication.

No sound came from inside his office, though, and she hazarded a few more steps, discovering a narrow hall with no apparent ending. Only a few emergency lights kept the corridor from being completely impossible to navigate. Finally, just as she'd expected, she found a passage leading downward, the door to it conspicuously ajar.

And this was where she stopped.

There were no more screams. Perhaps someone had tended to the unhappy girl and gotten her to sleep again. Jocelyn was practical enough to assume that meant a heavy dose of sedatives to get the job done. Her curiosity was piqued, certainly, but there was curiosity and then there was recklessness. Her first few weeks on the job had gone well—why jeopardize her position by poking around where she didn't belong?

Then the scream came again, longer, agonizing, twisting high and into a word.

"Please."

That was more than enough motivation for Jocelyn. She set her jaw, racing down the stairs without a second thought. Surely nobody could fault her—a nurse—for wanting to give a poor soul comfort and relief. There would be sedatives somewhere. She

could at least help the girl back to sleep and spare the other patients the distress of her cries.

And spare me *them, too.*

The emergency lighting grew thinner. Threadbare bulbs dangled above her head, the stairs going on and on, twisting, taking her far lower than she expected to go. Other corridors intersected, locked doors meeting up with the path downward. The air grew colder, damper, true subterranean clamminess making her sweater feel like tissue paper. Jocelyn rubbed her arms, determined but slowing, her steps less sure as she finally turned the last corner.

It wasn't so much a hallway as it was a very tall, long room. It ran straight forward into darkness, and the sensation of looking into a vanishing, narrow point tightened her stomach in nausea. Jocelyn passed under the archway, shivering as a sharp rush of air followed her through.

She squinted. What could possibly be down here? This didn't at all resemble the bright, clean storage rooms at Grace Point. She couldn't imagine a reason to keep anything, let alone *anyone*, in such a gloomy place.

Doors sprung up on either side of her, taller and more forbidding than those of the patient and dormitory levels above. Heavy, rusted hinges and grate-guarded windows, thick with grime, made her wonder if they were housing Dr. Moreau's failed creations and not troubled human beings.

It felt too cold, too silent to be a safe place for patients. Dead, almost.

Then the girl screamed again, and the rending sound was only muffled by one door, maybe two this time. And that scream

brought all the doors in the hall to life. They rattled, they shook, fists slamming on unrelenting metal, hinges groaning against the sudden savagery. More voices chorused with hers, cries and wails. Bellows. Laughter.

Out of the mayhem, a coherent refrain emerged: *"Help her, help her, help her."*

Slowly, a door opened farther down the hall, a pale shaft of light spilling onto the dirty floor. Jocelyn didn't wait to see who or what would come out. She silently cursed herself a coward, turned, and ran.

The girl is soft. Moldable. Like Dennis. Not as eager as Dennis, I'm sure, but few are. She is defiant and arrogant, but that defiance can be harnessed. God, I hesitate to say it, but she brings to mind a younger version of myself. Not as determined, not as naturally gifted, but I see flickers of my past, reminders of where I started and how far I have come. Her talents are wasted and she knows it, and that resentment is my way in. I see the seeds of great things in her, but I will need to approach her carefully. A demonstration is in order, one that will prove beyond a doubt that sometimes sickness really cannot be cured.

It hardly matters that the sickness is all my doing.

I believe I am still waiting on the best candidate to propel my research forward, but this will prove an amusing distraction until that time.

—Excerpt from Warden Crawford's journals—late April

CHAPTER № 3

*W*hat had she seen? And more important, what was she going to *do* about it?

She could leave her post for good, she realized, get back on a bus and go somewhere, anywhere else. But that would mean leaving all those people behind, and she would carry around their pleas for help for the rest of her life—not to mention Madge would be inconsolable. The guilt would eat away at her. She had come to be a nurse. To help.

And she knew exactly who to ask for clarification.

Sometimes the best way forward was the simplest. Medicine was a straightforward, noble science. That's what she liked about it. The goal was obvious—find the problem and then find the solution, and in doing so, help a patient return to a healthy life. The risk was great but the reward was even greater.

Warden Crawford would know what the basement was all about. He would give her the answers she needed. Explain how what she'd seen was part of a necessary risk.

But first, breakfast.

The staff cafeteria abutted the one where the more stable, low-risk patients ate. Jocelyn's eyes followed nurses zooming away from their bacon and eggs at a moment's notice to respond to some flare-up or scuffle in the other cafeteria, their white coats flapping like wings behind them as they went.

Across from her, Madge wolfed down an impressive stack of pancakes.

"I just have one of those bodies, you know," she said in between bites. "I can eat anything and never gain a pound."

"Mm." Jocelyn didn't mean to be rude, but she was firing on about two cylinders—which Madge had noticed, of course.

"You know what works so, so well?" she chirped, picking up her unused spoon and showing it to Jocelyn. "Stick some spoons in the icebox overnight, in the morning you put the round part on your eyes and voilà! No more puffiness."

"Subtle." She didn't share Madge's gusto for breakfast—or ordinarily she might, but this morning her mind was elsewhere. A few bites of oatmeal and a gulp of orange juice were all she could manage.

Madge scooted a cup of black coffee across the table.

"For if the spoons don't wake you up," she whispered with a wink.

"You ladies look chipper this morning."

Jocelyn glanced up from the coffee, her stomach souring in anticipation of its taste. The orderly she had caught sleeping in the dispensary was there, setting down his tray next to Madge. Setting it down very close to Madge's tray.

"Good morning, Tanner."

She shot Madge a look, eyebrow raised, as if to say, *That was fast.*

Madge gave a tiny, one-shouldered shrug and blushed.

"Joss, this is Tanner. Tanner, this is, well, Joss." She laughed, adorably, and Tanner started to turn red, too, as if they were even now laying the groundwork for some future inside joke.

He certainly looked like a Tanner—tall, with sandy blond hair swept meticulously to the side, an Ivy League athlete's body. . . . But there was a sweet sleepiness to his grayish blue eyes that convinced her he didn't have an aggressive bone in his body.

Jocelyn took a long swig of coffee and nodded. "I've seen you around, but it's nice to finally meet you properly."

"You, too. Welcome to Brookline," he said with a sigh. "It can be tough adjusting to life around here, especially if this is your first posting. If you have any problems, any questions, I'm always happy to help out. Some of the doctors get real grumpy if you ask for too much help. They like to seem up to their ears in work."

"Aren't they?" Jocelyn asked. She added a smile, not a convincing one, but he didn't notice.

"Oh sure," he replied. "But there's a hierarchy, you know? The warden is the warden, the doctors are the doctors. Almost like, um, almost like the army, in a way."

She nodded. She had sensed that already, but his words only confirmed who she needed to speak with first.

"I'm wondering if I should go darker with my hair," Madge mused aloud, looping a perfect coil of blond hair around her finger and quite effectively bringing the conversation back her way. "Jackie looks so dramatic with that black hair. So mysterious."

"Jackie?" Tanner had finally started on his breakfast and then abandoned it again to gawk at Madge.

"Kennedy, dummy."

"Oh, sure. Of course."

"Anyway, what do you think, Tanner? I think maybe I'll try to

find a salon in town. Do you think Camford even has one?" She laughed, slicing the last of her pancakes into perfect triangles.

"That would be a shame. I thought blondes had more fun, but . . . ," he said, far more interested in Madge's profile than he was in his scrambled eggs.

"They have more work, too," Madge said, frowning, flashing them both a delicate wristwatch. "Time for our shift. Wish us an easy one!"

"They're never easy," he said.

Eager to get started, Jocelyn popped up out of her seat, hoping nobody noticed that she had barely eaten her food or touched her coffee. Tanner's arm shot across the table, his hand catching around her wrist and holding until she made eye contact.

"What are you—"

"Hey, don't worry. Sleeping will get easier," he said firmly.

"What?" She knew there were circles under her eyes, but was it that obvious? Had he seen her sneaking around in the lobby? She had slept fine before; it was just the sudden screaming that made her look and feel like hell warmed over.

"I had trouble sleeping through the night when I first got here, too," Tanner added, releasing her wrist. He laughed, bitterly, shaking his head. "Damnedest thing. Kept thinking I was hearing things, but it went away after a while. If it keeps up, talk to Warden Crawford. He can give you something for it."

"What kind of something?" she asked, listening to Madge sigh with impatience behind her.

Tanner shrugged, turning back to his breakfast. "Didn't catch the label. Anyway it worked, and he's the doctor, right?"

CHAPTER
№ 4

*M*ost people hated the smell of hospitals, but not Jocelyn. In a way it was almost an absence of scent. Scrubbed air. The opposite of the exhaust-pipe-and-hot-dog-stand funk she was forced to gulp down in Chicago. She breathed the specific mix of cleaning agents—crisp, devoid of anything sour or musky—and let it fill her whole body with that calming sense of *right*. That smell meant miracles were happening all around her, and here, at Brookline, those miracles weren't hemorrhages being stemmed or heart medicine prescribed—here it meant ferrying patients from a broken mind to a whole one.

That almost seemed like a kind of magic.

Jocelyn forced herself to focus as their supervisor, Nurse Kramer, went over dispensary protocol with them in great detail. Apparently medicines were coming up short, and she wanted to give everyone a refresher on marking out what was used and what was thrown away. Soon after they would be released to work their shifts, but Jocelyn was alert, looking for an out. She wanted to speak to Warden Crawford alone, but she worried that what Tanner had said was true—that the warden wouldn't have time for her now that she was just one of the many worker bees in his hive.

So she trained her eyes on Nurse Kramer's plump,

baby-smooth face and listened as she reviewed the hospital's system for tracking medicines and sedatives distributed to patients, where to drop off samples, charts, notes. . . . Her skill for memorizing that kind of minutiae had proved useful in training, and it would prove useful again, she realized with a sigh, watching Madge twinkle her fingers at a passing Tanner.

"Nurse Fullerton, are we going to have a problem today?"

Madge snapped her head around, using the same big, fluffy lashes she used to ogle boys. "Charts there." She pointed. "Mark down each and every dosage with dotted *i*'s and crossed *t*'s, and Dr. Aimes has been having a bad reaction to dairy, so no milk if he asks for coffee."

"I didn't say anything about Dr. Aimes." Nurse Kramer's bubbly cheeks rippled with irritation.

Shrugging, Madge tucked her hands meekly behind her back. "Just a hunch."

"Nurse Fullerton is incredibly observant," Jocelyn put it mildly.

"Yes. So am I."

The girls went silent, falling into step behind the older nurse as she led them out of the tiny, many-cubbied room to the reception area and then the lobby. A nervous couple sat waiting near the magazines, holding hands but staring straight ahead. They flinched at the sight of the nurses, as if Jocelyn and her colleagues were a firing squad come to summon them to execution.

Nurse Kramer breezed by them with a placid smile fixed in place.

Mere steps from the corridor leading to the visitation and

diagnosis rooms, they were intercepted by Warden Crawford, his large frame blocking the hall as he precipitously headed them off. Nurse Kramer jumped and squeaked in surprise, then collected herself just as quickly. But Jocelyn noted the way she flushed, and the way that her eyes began to dart along the fringes of her vision. Odd. She would bet money that Nurse Kramer's heart rate had elevated, that her pupils were dilated.

Fear? Excitement? Why exactly did Nurse Kramer have so much trouble meeting his eye?

"Good morning, Nurse Kramer. Nurse Fullerton. Nurse Ash." He turned to Jocelyn, snapping his heels together as he did so. In contrast to his office, his clothes were immaculate. His patent leather shoes practically glowed. "I need to steal Nurse Ash momentarily. I trust that won't be a great imposition."

"N-no. No, of course not, sir. Nurse Ash, you will go now, please."

Her tone had taken a sudden dive into severe, almost challenging, as if she expected Jocelyn to refuse. Which Jocelyn didn't. This was exactly what she wanted, after all. But now that he was looming in front of them, the full force of his attention trained on her, she began to lose confidence in her plan. The future of her job rested in his hands, and if she caused a fuss she could be out of work by the afternoon.

You know what you saw. You deserve an explanation. The patients deserve one.

"Right away, sir, lead the way," she said brightly, channeling Madge but feeling anything but sunshine on the inside.

Jocelyn stared at the porcelain head sculpture on Warden Crawford's desk. The regions of the brain were mapped and labeled,

neat black script painted across the top of the skull, borders clearly defined as if the mind were a series of nations.

Her gaze strayed back to him as he touched his fingertips to his temples and rubbed. His office looked marginally cleaner today. Perhaps a maid had been in to straighten.

"You needed to speak to me?" she prompted, stiff. Her skin prickled with cold; it was like being called to the head of the class, scolded, shamed. . . . But why would he scold her? She hadn't done anything wrong.

You know why.

Warden Crawford fixed her with an unblinking stare, deepening her conviction that she was about to be unceremoniously sacked. The thought ought to unnerve her more, but a thin strain of reason insisted she would be glad to be away from this place. Except that would be selfish—something was wrong here and she would be a coward to turn her back.

"This may seem premature, Nurse Ash. . . ."

Jocelyn braced. Here it was. She was definitely getting fired.

"But I'm selecting you for a special program. An experimental program."

She blinked at him robotically in response. Either she was hearing things or she wasn't getting fired, she was getting a kind of promotion. "I . . . beg your pardon, sir?"

He laughed, a warm, curious laugh that reminded her of being a child, of being affectionately indulged. The warden plucked off his spectacles and then rubbed them on the bottom of his white coat. Pulling a small tin from his pocket, he flicked it open with his thumbnail and popped a mint into his mouth.

"Want one?" he asked, offering the tin to her across the desk.

Jocelyn shook her head, still a little dazed. So that was where the sharp, spearmint smell came from. His office smelled different from the rest of the floor, free of that clean, antiseptic hospital smell she liked so much.

"No, thank you. I'm still . . . I guess I'm still wondering what you mean by special program? What exactly would that involve? I mean, I haven't even gotten into a routine here."

Warden Crawford put up a hand, tucking the mints away and nodding. She could tell from the soft sucking sounds and the distortion of his cheeks that he was flipping the mint around in his mouth. "Sit, please. I sprang that on you too soon, I know."

She did sit, grateful for the grounding presence of the chair underneath her.

Propping his elbows on the desk, he sat, too, the porcelain skull with its territories of the mind centered between them as if there to mediate or observe. "Do you know how one comes to be in charge of a place like this?"

Jocelyn did, in the vaguest sense. She had studied the career path herself, dreaming a dream she knew was utterly ridiculous in the eyes of most. The Warden didn't need to know that. Damn. He was drawing her away from the topic she actually wanted to discuss. But maybe accepting this new position would make her more valuable in his eyes. If she could become a trusted employee, then maybe he might be more amenable to addressing the strange situation in the basement more openly.

"I do," she said, risking: "But we're not exactly encouraged to strive for that ourselves."

"Ah. You mean as a young woman. Yes. I quite understand. Archaic, really, that manner of thinking. Most of our colleagues

229

would insist a woman's compassion makes her immanently suited for caretaking professions, but we both know this work demands a degree of coldness, of distance that stands directly at odds with that belief."

Jocelyn couldn't help but agree, remembering the last, painful days with her grandmother, when implementing that kind of distance was the only thing that had gotten her through. She nodded slowly, hoping he wasn't drawing her into a trap, making her trip and stick her foot in her mouth. Maybe he wanted to know if he had uppity, defiant girls operating in his institution.

She said, "There will always be patients who are beyond our help, even if it's awful to say so."

His eyes seemed to glow at her words, and he lowered his head slightly, sighting her like a predator might their prey.

"You honestly believe that?" he asked.

"I . . ." Jocelyn trusted her gut, straightening and saying firmly, "Yes, I do. Some people cannot be cured. Not really. And it's a misuse of hospital resources to insist otherwise."

"You . . . you're clever." He wagged a finger at her, that strange light still filling his eyes. "Exactly as I suspected—you're the right choice for this new program."

"*What* new program?" Jocelyn asked, perhaps too sharply. "What would I be doing?"

"That's complicated, Nurse Ash. As I said, it's experimental, and it's to do with exactly what you just expressed so eloquently— that some people cannot be helped. I am of the same mind, but I'd take it a step further. Some patients are beyond help, but they are not beyond *use*."

She stilled. *Use?* That felt like an odd choice of words.

"How do you mean?" she asked, shifting.

The warden wiped off his spectacles on his coat again and tucked them into his pocket. Then he stood, placing his knuckles on the desk and looming over it, leaning toward her. His shadow fell across the skull statue, spilling over files and papers and then onto her lap.

"What did you see in the basement, Nurse Ash?" he asked. "Or should I say, what do you *think* you saw?"

Of all the scenarios Jocelyn had considered the night before and that morning, ending up back in the basement with Warden Crawford was not one. Fired? Sure. Lectured? Most definitely. This was, theoretically, the best outcome. So why did her blood feel icy and sluggish in her veins? The trip down felt shorter this time, probably because Warden Crawford obviously knew the way, and the stairwell was well lit in the daytime.

Was she completely mad? It looked so harmless, so normal, like this. Maybe the shadows and her own anxieties had altered her perspective. This was totally possible—she knew enough about the field of psychology to understand that context and one's own fears could change something harmless into a threat.

She followed her superior closely, as if afraid she might stumble into a wrong turn and never find her way out again. Just as she remembered, the bottom level was uncomfortably cold, the tall, foreboding archway ushering them toward the corridor with its many doors. The screams were absent this time. No doors rattled. In fact, a few orderlies wandered the corridor, clipboards in hand, trays laden with small cups of water and pills. They smiled distractedly at her as they passed.

"I didn't mean to snoop," Jocelyn suddenly said. She had apologized already in his office after the accusation that she had been to the basement. The correct accusation. The warden had waved off her apology then, just like he shrugged her off now.

"Curiosity is natural," he replied casually. "But your response is perhaps not."

"You don't know that." She was pushing too far again. That would get her into trouble, she knew, if she wasn't careful.

"You showed up to work this morning," the warden pointed out. "As far as I know, you said nothing to anyone, despite witnessing something rather *unorthodox*."

"I didn't understand why patients were put down here—I still don't—and frankly I was going to ask you about it today. In your office."

"Well, this should suffice for an explanation, then, mm?"

Jocelyn watched the doors going by, shocked by how many there really were. The daylight hours did nothing to banish the sad, abandoned ugliness of this lowest level. The staff could paint the walls yellow and put teddy bears in every corner and it would still feel like a hidden, shameful hell. The damp remained oppressive during the day, and while the floor was swept, it didn't at all measure up to the rigorous hygiene standards of other hospitals.

And the hospital smell was gone. She hadn't noticed it until now, but all at once it became offensively apparent. There was a distinctly unwashed-human-being smell that wafted in intervals from the closed doors, like the rooms were ovens, heating up bodies and churning out their humid sweat stench.

"Basements. Experiments. I'm not sure I like this," Jocelyn

said. She stuck her hands into the pockets of the clean, tailored coat buttoned tightly around her. "Are these the most trouble-some patients?"

"They are, yes." The warden paused outside a door toward the end of the corridor. He rocked up onto his toes and pulled open a slot in the door, peering inside before producing a giant set of keys from his pocket. "They have resisted known treat-ments. I never would have said this when I was just a young, green orderly, but some of them seem to *prefer* their madness."

"That's not possible," Jocelyn said, frowning. "It's a prison they don't even know they're in, how could they prefer it?"

"Perhaps it's an intuition that comes with age and experi-ence," he replied, unlocking the door. "You'll see."

I doubt that.

But she kept her mouth shut, aware that she was sliding closer to the answers she wanted out of him. Why hide these people away? Were the orderlies down here part of his strange new project? And just what did he expect from her. . . .

She could still leave, she reminded herself. Jocelyn still hadn't technically agreed to be part of his new program. As she stepped through the open door and into the room beyond, she noticed Warden Crawford watching her intently, scrutinizing her for the tiniest reaction.

The room, small but tall, padded floor to ceiling, resonated with cold. A single window let in a pale shaft of sunlight from high, high above, with bars obscuring the view, just like in her room. Jocelyn took a single step into the room, trying to orient herself. That window probably looked out the same way hers did. She slept the night before floors and floors up, possibly situated

on top of this very cell. And taking one look at the patient inside, a baby-bird fragile girl in a threadbare nightgown, Jocelyn knew she was the one who had roused her with screams.

"Do . . . do you have her chart?" Jocelyn asked. She spoke softly, afraid to startle the girl.

"You can review it later."

"I'd like to review it now," Jocelyn said, turning and standing to face him. "I shouldn't even be here with her, not without knowing her history."

"I'm giving you special permission." She heard the irritation, the *impatience*, in his voice.

The girl, previously facing away from them, finally noticed their presence. She turned, slowly, bare feet slapping on the floor as she shuffled around, arms at her sides, hair darkened with grease and grime hanging lank down her back.

"These conditions . . ." Jocelyn began, stuffing down an urge to spin and throttle the man behind her. How could he let a human being live like this? It wasn't right. Her stomach turned, her whole body rebelling at the sight of the poor, neglected girl.

"You want to help her," Warden Crawford observed.

"Yes. Yes, of course I do. Don't you?" She pinned him with a helpless look. The girl now stood motionless, pale and unnatural as porcelain.

"And how would you help her, Nurse Ash?"

He had sidestepped the question, but Jocelyn had more important things on her mind. "Bathe her, for one. Dress her in warmer clothing. House her in a place fit for humans. My God, I wouldn't keep a rabid dog in here."

He had the grace to flinch at that assessment of his facility.

But then he was taking the spectacles out of his pocket and placing them serenely back on his nose. He didn't seem to notice the girl, and when his eyes chanced in her direction he only looked *through* her.

"Then help her."

Jocelyn knew it couldn't be as simple as all that, but she never backed down from a challenge. This was a thrown gauntlet, and she would pick it up, if only to prove that it was never right to give up on a person, especially one so young.

Her own foolish words came back to haunt her.

Some people cannot be cured. Not really. And it's a misuse of hospital resources to insist otherwise.

This was different. This was a child. Jocelyn drummed up her courage and turned to face the young girl, but she dropped the stern expression on her face, approaching with extreme caution. As a child she had always thought nurses looked so kindly and innocent, like guardian angels in their clean white uniforms. Angels were not always so good, Jocelyn knew that. She had read the Bible. But she was not an avenging angel today— no, this poor little bird needed to be cupped in warm hands and brought back to a nest. She was a tumbled sparrow, something to be treated gently and with ultimate care.

Jocelyn crouched, holding out her hand to the fragile child.

"Here now, little birdy, little sparrow. Why don't you come here to me? You look awfully cold. Wouldn't a warm bath be nice?"

The girl hesitated, eyes shifting from the floor to Jocelyn's face and back again. Her eyes were black marbles, colorless pits.

"What's your name, sweetheart?" Jocelyn asked, letting her hand fall to her side.

Warden Crawford didn't wait for her to answer. "Lucy. Her name is Lucy."

Lucy's dark eyes found focus, gliding from Jocelyn to the man behind her. Speaking her name was like a curse, a spell. Suddenly she lunged forward, blindly, fingers unexpectedly strong and curved into talons. She tore at whatever was in her path, and that happened to be Jocelyn. Dodging, flailing, Jocelyn just managed to avoid one of those hooked hands coming for her eye and grabbed the girl around the waist, twisting and holding her, doing what she could to pin her arms.

She heard Warden Crawford take one resolute step backward.

If this was the first test, Jocelyn would not give up. She tried again, coaxing the girl's arms down to her sides and holding them fast. This did little to deter Lucy in her rage. She wriggled and bucked, hurling herself back and forth until the force of it was too much for Jocelyn.

She fled, releasing the girl and retreating to the door. But Lucy didn't follow. Instead, she tore around the room, spinning, pulling at her own hair, knocking herself against the walls until she was breathless and panting.

Jocelyn paused on the threshold of the room, feeling helpless. *Smash. Smash. Smash.* With every brutal toss of her body against the wall the girl was saying something, whispering it, hissing it out in a slice of a whisper.

It took Jocelyn a moment to catch the word, hearing it cleanly just as the warden tugged her out by the shoulder and closed the door.

✗ ✗ ✗ ✗ ✗

"Do you still want to help her?"

It was a ridiculous question. Jocelyn ground her teeth together as she followed Warden Crawford back through the basement and toward the staircase leading up.

"Yes. Naturally."

"You saw how she reacted to the mere suggestion of a bath," he replied, taking another mint from his tin and eating it before starting up the stairs. He walked with his hands tucked behind his back. It struck her as indecently casual, given what they had just witnessed.

But that was a doctor's life, she reminded herself. If every wound or tantrum or spot of blood knocked them off their post, nothing would ever get done.

"I think she reacted to you, or to her name," Jocelyn replied. "I'm sorry if it's offensive to say so."

Warden Crawford shrugged. "Not at all. Lucy is a strange case. Her parents swear up and down that she has no history of abuse. That one day she simply stopped speaking. They took her to specialists—speech therapists, hypnotists, you name it, they tried it. Then the outbursts began. Silent, furious storms not unlike what you just observed."

"That was anything but silent," Jocelyn murmured, hugging herself.

"The screaming didn't begin until she came here. Her muteness persists between episodes, then something causes the hysterical fits. Men, usually. She is mostly docile if only nurses see to her. Bathing and clothing her remain . . . challenging."

Jocelyn paused on the landing, feeling the dread atmosphere of the basement slip off her like chilled silk. "Then why did you

go into that room? You deliberately wanted to frighten her?"

He stared back at her evenly, one eyebrow cocked in amusement or irritation. "Perhaps. Perhaps I wanted you to see just what you're up against."

"And this is all part of your . . . your *program*?"

"Lucy and the others in basement confinement are difficult cases. Traditional methods have proven ineffective, counterproductive, even. Medicine must march forward, Nurse Ash. Surely you understand that." He turned, assuming she would follow. He continued, "We could sedate Lucy, true. She could live out a long, wasted life in a stupor, or we could do what others will not."

A hard shiver raced down Jocelyn's spine. "You want to experiment on her."

"You make it sound so dreadfully Frankensteinian," he said with a chuckle. They had reached the lobby level and he held the door for her. Jocelyn flinched, afraid even to get too near to him. "Most leaps forward happen by pure accident. What I'm suggesting is far more methodical. Hypnotism, surgery, drug therapy . . . These techniques are often used independently of one another, but I foresee a future in which we can control and guide these patients back to productive living through an aggressive combination of all three."

He led her swiftly back to his office, and again she ducked past him into the room, curious and listening despite herself. "Why hasn't this been done before?"

"Cowardice?" Warden Crawford suggested, sauntering behind his desk and dropping down into his chair. "Lack of vision? Fear of failure? Take your pick, I suppose. We stand on the cusp, Nurse Ash, and to be the vanguard we must be bold."

"I . . . I don't know."

"Would it help if I asked Nurse Fullerton to participate, too?" he asked gently. "She seems capable enough. Perhaps between the two of you, you can keep me in check. Two heads are better than one, and three is certainly better still."

His smile was wide, movie-star white. For a moment he almost looked boyish. His face defied the look of a true age, as if he was hovering always between adolescence and adulthood. Timeless, her mother would say. Madge would probably say it, too.

Something gnawed at the edge of her subconscious. Jocelyn cleared her throat softly and asked, "What was she saying? Lucy, I mean. That word she kept saying . . . What does it mean?"

His smile collapsed in on itself. "Nonsense, I imagine. We have patients here who have made up entire languages to confound."

It sounded like Spanish. It didn't sound made up at all.

The thin remnants of his smile cracked with impatience at the edges. Jocelyn weighed her options quickly—there was always leaving, of course, but she worried about leaving Madge alone. And now she worried about Lucy. The girl was human like anyone else and she deserved a better life than she was getting at Brookline. If Jocelyn could improve it, she would, and if the warden insisted on trying to cure Lucy with newfangled ideas, Jocelyn would be there to make sure he didn't do more harm than good.

First, do no harm. And second, make sure nobody else does harm either.

"All right," she said quickly. "I'll do it." She swallowed around

a golf ball–sized lump of anxiety in her throat. "When do we begin?"

"Tomorrow, I think," Warden Crawford said cheerfully. He winked. "After you tell Nurse Fullerton the good news."

✗ ✗ ✗ ✗ ✗

The path is set down. I have already instructed the cooks and provided them with the necessary embellishments. I know the treatment works on the vulnerable, it will be exciting to see if it similarly affects the whole of mind. Though really, it is debatable how whole that ninny's mind truly is. No matter. She will be the perfect demonstration—Lucy is tragic, yes, but to witness a fall from sound to unsound? To be powerless to stop such degradation? It will bring the girl around and it will sharpen her into a fine tool for my use.

—Excerpt from Warden Crawford's journals—April

"This isn't the Serengeti, Madge. Stop hunting."

Madge batted her eyelashes and shrugged, pouting about as innocently as a kid with her hand still fully submerged in the cookie jar.

"I have no idea to what you could be referring," she said, bumping her hip against Jocelyn's as they organized charts in the nurses' station. It was monotonous work, but crucial to keep the schedules running efficiently.

"First Tanner and now . . ." Jocelyn groped for the young orderly's name, blushing. She had a quick mind, but not the best memory for names and faces. He was handsome, that much was obvious, and he had just sidled away from the station while giving Madge a heated, hooded-eyed smolder.

"Oh, David," Madge purred. "He's just a friend, I swear."

Jocelyn paused, cocking her head to the side. Again, her subconscious flared, whispering the word that had followed her from the basement to her rounds to her bed that night. She had started chanting it to herself silently to keep from forgetting.

"Look, I know this is a long shot, but are you still in touch with that guy you used to go with back home? He was Spanish or something, right?" she asked.

"Puerto Rican," Madge corrected, a little sharply.

"Do you two still talk?"

"Lord, no," Madge said with a giggle. "Where'd that come from? I haven't thought of Armando in months."

Jocelyn shrugged, picking at her fingernails. "I just thought maybe you could ask him something for me. There's this word in Spanish I've been trying to figure out. At least I think it's Spanish. . . ."

"Well, geez, that's no trouble. I learned quite a bit just from getting to know the guy," Madge replied with a grin. She tapped a few folders on the countertop, squaring them off. "It's such a good language for seduction."

Jocelyn finished her portion of the alphabet, her eyes scanning involuntarily for Lucy's name. She didn't see anything; maybe the girl's information was in Madge's half of the stack.

"Nothing like that. I just heard a word yesterday that I couldn't place. It sounded like *carnee . . . carnay-zero*? *Carnaysarah* . . . God, I'm hopeless at this."

"Yuck, I hope that wasn't someone talking about your bedside manner," Madge teased. She tapped her hip against Jocelyn's again. "*Carnicero*. It means butcher. You didn't stick their vein wrong with a needle, did you?"

Jocelyn forgot to answer. Butcher. *Butcher*. And Lucy had started screaming it immediately after Warden Crawford spoke her name. . . . Jocelyn felt suddenly queasy. Madge had already been called into his office that morning and agreed to help participate in this "program" of his without question. What the hell had Jocelyn gotten them into? It was too late to leave now, she knew, because if she did she would forever worry about what had happened to Lucy. If she had gotten better, or if the warden had kept her down in that dank cell until the cold and the darkness consumed her.

"Hello? *Jocelyn?* Was it the tuna fish at lunch? Lord, I swear it was off. Mine tasted fishy. Well, *bad* fishy, not tuna fishy like it ought to. You need the toilet?"

Jocelyn shook her head, her mouth dry and tasteless. "No. Just . . . Yeah, maybe I do need a moment."

"Told ya. Cafeteria tuna fish will get you every damn time. I got the rest of this, you scoot your boot out of here. I just bought these shoes and you are not dousing them in something foul."

The water on her face felt like the cold slap of reality. Even if it brought her out of her daze momentarily, it didn't change how the face staring back at her in the mirror was almost unrecognizable. Two days of minimal sleep and maximum stress had turned her usually glossy strawberry-colored hair dull and limp. The skin under her eyes was thin and bluish, veins visible through the unhealthy pallor.

Jocelyn pulled at her cheeks, moving the flesh along her face until the pressing and prodding hurt. It wasn't the tuna making her feel ill, she knew, she had hardly touched her food since arriving. She braced her hands on the cold, white sink and sighed. It had to change.

Pushing away from the sink, she let the spark of an idea catch fire and spread. It was risky, sure, maybe even stupid, but Jocelyn refused to be helpless. She had agreed to help Warden Crawford, but that didn't mean she was above trying a few unorthodox methods of her own.

She stormed out of the bathroom and back down the hall,

passing Tanner the orderly as she went. That changed her idea slightly, but only for the better. She skidded to a halt on her practical heels and spun, managing to hook her hand around his elbow.

He had been checking off the list of rooms to be aired out and cleaned, and his head jerked up at her hand latching on to him. "Hey. Whoa. Need something?"

Jocelyn nodded, shooting a quick look down the hall to make sure they weren't being watched. There was nothing but the soft murmur of patients in their rooms farther down the corridor to her left and Madge's idle whistling from the nurses' station to the right.

"Can you get access to a wheelchair?"

"I . . . think so, yes. Why do you ask?" He studied her over his thick-rimmed glasses, lips quirked to the side.

"Would you get one for me even if I said I couldn't explain right away?"

That made him take a longer pause.

"It's for Madge, too," she said.

And that did the trick.

"All right. All right, sure, why not? Do you need it now?" he asked, lowering his clipboard.

"Meet us at the top of the stairwell around the corner, the one that goes to the basement. We'll be right back, I promise!" With that she took off at a swift clip, keeping an eye out for Nurse Kramer or any of the doctors on staff. And especially for Warden Crawford. She poked her head into the nurses' station, finding Madge bopping along to her own whistling rendition of Top 40 songs.

"Hey! I've got an idea. Come with me. . . ."

"Where are we going?" Madge asked, but she was clearly game, her yellow curls bouncing along as she hurried after Jocelyn toward the lobby and the connecting hall.

Jocelyn pressed her finger to her lips, tiptoeing past Warden Crawford's office. His silhouette was visible, pacing within. She took Madge by the wrist and carefully pulled her along, cautiously opening the door to the basement stairwell before dashing down the first set of stairs.

"Ugh. Crawford took me down here this morning," Madge muttered, sticking out her tongue. "Beyond gross."

"Did he take you to see Lucy?" she whispered.

"What? No. Who's that? He took me to this patient Dennis. Kept talking about the White Mountains. 'White Mountains, so beautiful, so still. The White Mountains, you would look so beautiful in the White Mountains.' I mean, what do you even say to that?"

"Was he violent?" Jocelyn asked, checking the way behind them as they reached the landing and then began descending again.

"Not that I saw, but Crawford wouldn't let me get too close to him."

They reached the basement level, cool, damp air rushing out to meet them from the patient corridor. It felt like a warning. But Jocelyn wasn't stopping now. She marched Madge along, still holding tight to her wrist.

"Did you see his chart? His history? Medications?"

WARDEN CRAWFORD

"No, nothing like that," Madge admitted with a sigh. "Honestly, Joss, the only reason I agreed to this 'program' is because you're doing it."

"I didn't see Lucy's either."

"Didn't see her what?" Madge asked, hesitating at the archway before the hall.

"Her history. Not previous procedures or medications. Nothing. It's giving me the willies, Madge. Why won't he show us? He's hiding something."

"He has to show us eventually, right?"

Jocelyn didn't have an answer for that. The same handful of orderlies Jocelyn had seen last time patrolled the corridor, their interest falling quickly on the two girls. Jocelyn dredged up the lie quickly, hoping it wasn't too clumsy. The nearest orderly, a tall, thin man with graying hair and a chin that disappeared into his neck, stopped them a few feet past the arch.

What if only Warden Crawford had keys to the patient rooms? What if the orderlies were just there to keep nosy girls like her away? It was too late not to at least ask, she reasoned, mimicking one of Madge's most brilliant smiles.

"Warden Crawford sent us down to fetch Lucy. He wants to examine her in Theater Twelve."

The orderly squinted, his beady eyes growing beadier. "I wasn't told about this."

"Last minute . . . last minute adjustment to his schedule. A family canceled their visit," Jocelyn lied wildly, nudging Madge in the ribs.

"Yes. Visit," Madge stammered. "They canceled it. Very sad."

Apparently Madge was an even worse liar, if it was possible.

"Do you want to keep him waiting?" Jocelyn pressed, frowning. "I don't think you do."

The orderly scrunched up his nose, giving them each a long, hard look before spinning on his heel and stomping back toward Lucy's room. Jocelyn closed her eyes tightly in relief; that had been a close one, and she had little faith that their luck would hold. This would get back to Crawford, and she could only pray that he would be lenient when he found out.

Or he'll fire you. Right? That's the worst thing he could do? "I'm glad we, um, don't have to keep the warden waiting," Madge said, trying on a no-nonsense nurse voice that nearly made Jocelyn giggle.

"I heard ya the first time, lady. I'm going as fast as I can," the orderly muttered, taking a set of keys from his pocket and flipping through them. "Sheesh."

It wasn't fast enough for Jocelyn, who couldn't help whipping her head around to make sure Crawford wasn't there, breathing down their necks. The other orderlies watched them, curious, and her nerves began to twitch again. Why were they staring like that? And why couldn't this idiot hurry up and just find the right key. . . .

Her pulse only raced faster as he unlocked Lucy's door and swung it open. They had come to the part of the plan Jocelyn hadn't wanted to consider at all. What if Lucy fought them too hard? What if Jocelyn couldn't get her to leave the room without having another episode?

But she wouldn't allow the orderly to see her worry. Instead, she breezed through the door, Madge following, and then slowed when she found Lucy standing in the middle of the room, alert, eyes wide, as if she had been waiting for them.

"Hello again, Lucy," Jocelyn said gently. "I'm here to take you upstairs, all right? Will you come along with us?"

To her surprise, Lucy jumped forward, practically sprinting out of the room. On the way, she took Jocelyn and Madge by the hands, her grip strong for her size and condition.

"That was easy," Madge murmured, taking a quick glance back as they hurried down the corridor.

"Would you want to stay in that cell?" Jocelyn whispered back. "She must be desperate for air."

CHAPTER № 6

*L*ucy almost spoiled the plot right after they reached the main level.

For a moment, Jocelyn was certain Tanner had abandoned them, but then he came around the corner, wheelchair gleaming like a chariot, and Jocelyn felt a spike of hope. Unfortunately, that hope was immediately dashed as they crossed in front of Crawford's office. Lucy recognized the name or the door, seizing in their grasp, her mouth opening wide in horror.

Jocelyn anticipated the scream just in time, clapping her hand over Lucy's mouth and wrestling her down into the wheelchair.

"No, no, no," she whispered. "Not him. We're not going to see him. Tanner, go!"

"Go *where*?"

"The lobby, the doors! Take her outside!"

"*Outside!?*" Madge hiss-whispered, trotting after Jocelyn and Tanner. The wheelchair squeaked as they turned it around and raced down the corridor, through the lobby, past the bewildered nurses at the station, and toward the front doors. "You're going to get us fired, Joss!"

"Relax, it's just for a minute, just so she can get some air and see the sky," Jocelyn replied, sounding much more calm and confident than she felt.

For her part, Lucy was behaving, sitting quietly, her hands clutching the handles of the wheelchair for dear life but her mouth clamped shut. Good. They might actually make it out the doors without the whole of Brookline being alerted.

Jocelyn dodged around the wheelchair, breaking into a run and reaching the doors before Tanner could crash into them. Flinging the doors wide, she couldn't help but smile, absorbing the look of wonder and excitement that broke across Lucy's face as the sunshine fell in her lap.

"Is there a point to this?" Madge asked, watching as Tanner wheeled the girl down the walkway and toward a shaded patch just to the right of the hospital. They paused near a bed of tulips, the flowers all bowed from so many nights of rain, but a few petals still clinging on. "Other than getting us all sacked, of course . . ."

"Isn't the 'program' all about unorthodox treatments?" Jocelyn said with a shrug. "Maybe she just needed some fresh air. It couldn't hurt."

"Yes, it could," Madge replied. "What if she runs off and we can't catch her?"

"There's a fence."

"What if it's . . . I don't know, overstimulating or something!? What if she has a deathly allergy to tulips? Or grass? What if she catches pneumonia and *dies*?"

"Man, are you always this square?" Tanner teased. He smiled at them, apparently enjoying the little jailbreak, his blue eyes gleaming behind his specs. "We take patients outside all the time for therapeutic walks. It's not that unusual, Madge."

"You do not get to call me square and then pretend we're on

a first-name basis!" she squawked, pacing. Her red, red lips turned down in a pout, but then she stopped, observing Lucy from the side as the girl simply sat in the wheelchair, kicking her gangly legs out, the bottoms of her feet brushing the grass. "Fine, I can admit she looks . . . better."

"Not so square then," Tanner said with a smirk.

"How do you feel, Lucy?" Jocelyn asked. She ignored the ga-ga looks the other two started giving each other. She couldn't imagine how anyone found a hospital setting romantic. And she didn't expect an answer from Lucy, but she asked anyway, going to crouch in front of the wheelchair and look up at the girl.

Lucy's big, black eyes swept the unkempt yard, taking in the fence, the trees, the wisps of fog that rolled up toward the grounds from the picturesque town below. It was impossible to tell what she might be thinking, but at least she wasn't screaming.

Jocelyn carefully, slowly, put out her hand, waiting to see if Lucy flinched or recoiled. But the girl did nothing, simply watched the nurse's hand get nearer and nearer, and then she closed her eyes as Jocelyn tucked a piece of lank hair behind the girl's ear.

She would call that progress.

"There now," Jocelyn said. "I think we can do a lot together, Lucy. I think we can help each other. You don't have to say anything, all right? Nobody expects you to say anything."

"*Carnicero.*"

Jocelyn blinked. The other two fell silent, too.

"The butcher," Jocelyn said softly, watching Lucy nod. "You . . . you think someone in Brookline is a butcher?"

"*Sí. Usted sabe el carnicero. El carnicero de Brookline.*" Her voice was high, prim.

Jocelyn gradually shifted her eyes to Madge, who swallowed noisily and said, "Yes, you know the butcher. The butcher of Brookline. That's . . . that's what she said, Joss."

Jocelyn turned back to Lucy to inquire further, but the girl had reached for Jocelyn's hand, taking it and holding it firmly between her two small, cold palms. Even the sunlight didn't seem to warm her skin to above freezing.

"He wants to cut open my head," the girl told her, her voice lightly accented. "He wants to cut it open and scoop out what's inside."

"Lucy, I really don't think that's true," Jocelyn said. "But I'm glad you're speaking to me. That's very brave of you, and I'm really, really proud. Does being outside make you feel better? I know it makes me feel better."

Lucy narrowed her eyes, studying Jocelyn as if she were a piteously stupid creature. It made Jocelyn feel small, it made her feel like Lucy was much, much older, impossibly older, a soul that had seen and done things Jocelyn couldn't even fathom.

Lucy released her hand, placing her own hands back on the wheelchair armrests. "Don't let him cut open my head," she said. "And now I would like to go back inside."

An act of rebellion. Perfect. I could hardly devise a better wedge to drive them apart. A minor inconvenience has been smoothed over—my supplies have run low over the years since my initial training, and I feared the supplements might dry up

for good. But where there is a will there is a way, and where there is a need there is greed. Trax Corp. will do nicely for now, so long as they prove a discreet and reliable partner.

More exciting still, the patient I have been waiting for has presented himself. Years of anticipation leading to this moment and I can hardly describe the feeling. Elation. Relief. Patient Zero has surfaced and now my work truly begins.

—Excerpt from Warden Crawford's journals—May

CHAPTER
№ 7

*T*he hammer blow of punishment never fell. Still, Jocelyn waited for it. She waited for days. She went to bed jittery and rose from restless sleep in a fog, so distracted that even Mrs. Small in the grips of her dementia noticed and commented on her demeanor. During breakfast she heard the whispers of the nurses as they gossiped about the now infamous jailbreak, keeping their distance so as not to be implicated, but none of them were ever called to Warden Crawford's office for discipline.

When he mentioned it, he simply referred to it as "that little incident" and carried on.

It made Jocelyn sick with anxiety, and it also made her realize that she really had been trying to get them all fired. It was sabotage of the most obvious kind, and it had gone completely ignored.

Jocelyn sat on her bed before another full day, braiding her hair into one plait before looping it into a bun and pinning it. The spring rain had started up again, softer now that a few weeks had gone by and May was approaching. Madge stood at her wardrobe, picking out a pair of nylons for the day.

"This poor little thing," Jocelyn said, finishing with her hair and reaching over to the bedside table for the cracked Minnie

258

Mouse statue. "Did I tell you? I broke this the first night we were here. You slept right through it."

She had even asked Nurse Kramer if she could borrow some of the patient craft supplies to fix the chip, but she was told curtly that "Therapeutic arts and crafts materials are *not* for frivolous use."

Somehow she got the feeling that if any other nurse had asked, the request would have been granted.

"Mm. I think you told me that."

"That's it? Usually I get an earful for telling you something twice." She laughed, but it died slowly as she looked from the figurine to her friend. Before, she hadn't really given a thought to how Madge picked out her nylons, but now she watched more closely, realizing that Madge had picked up each clean pair in succession, held it briefly, and then put it back. She repeated the same odd ritual three more times before Jocelyn finally spoke up.

"Maybe we should get to bed earlier," she suggested, putting Minnie back on the table and standing. She smoothed down the front of her uniform. "You're practically sleepwalking."

"Am I?"

Jocelyn frowned, joining her friend at the wardrobe and picking up a pair of plain, nude nylons. "These are fine. The ones with the seam up the back just seem a little . . . racy. Save those for date night."

"Fine," Madge said, ripping the nylons out of her grasp. "We should get down to breakfast. I'm half-starved."

Jocelyn nodded, retreating to the door while her friend finished dressing. She had tried not to notice the change in Madge, who treated Jocelyn so similarly to the way the other nurses treated her now. Taking Lucy on that wheelchair ride had made Jocelyn a pariah, but she never expected to feel it from Madge, too. The change might have been subtle, but she felt it. How could she not? Madge was her only ally in the place. It did seem like it wasn't just an attitude shift. . . . Madge seemed to be smoking more, popping out for more frequent breaks, and she carried around a little package of lozenges everywhere, chewing them constantly, sometimes so loudly it made Jocelyn want to climb up the walls.

The one time she asked for one, Madge shot her a glare and flatly refused.

At least Tanner still spoke to her occasionally.

Everyone here is so wonderful, Mom. Just so warm. Kind, really. You'd be so proud of how Madge and I are doing. The warden has taken a shine to us, and I think this points to a bright future for us both.

She winced at the memory of writing to her family. Three drafts ended up crumpled, torn, and thrown under the bed because they told the truth. Even writing it all out had felt strangely cathartic—the long hours, the strange requests that they filled for Warden Crawford (sit with the patients between these hours and these hours, use these words with them but not these, give them exactly this kind of food), the secrets, the pervasive cold of the basement, the violent, screaming episodes. . . .

But Jocelyn couldn't bring herself to send those letters. Her mother would worry, and Jocelyn couldn't have that.

There was one bright spot to write about at least, she thought with a half smile: Lucy had seriously improved in the last few weeks. Crawford had even encouraged Jocelyn to take the girl outside a few more times, and as long as he stayed out of sight, the time out of doors seemed to soothe and bolster the child, even if she had never spoken another word after that first trip.

Jocelyn roused herself from her thoughts, finding Madge had put on her nylons and heels and moved to the bedside table. Holding the Minnie Mouse figure, she swayed almost imperceptibly back and forth.

"Madge? We should get going, don't you think?"

Madge's bouncy blond curls shot up as she inhaled and placed the figurine back on the table. "I was just looking at her. She reminded me of our trip to Disneyland when I was nine."

"I didn't know you went to Disneyland," Jocelyn said, grinning. "I've always wanted to go. It sounds so magical."

"It was," Madge said, smiling herself at the memory as she followed Jocelyn out of their room and into the hall. "It was. I climbed on a bench because a crowd was forming around Mickey. My father told me to stay still and be patient but I couldn't. I climbed onto a bench for a better look. I remember him saying, 'Careful, doll, you'll fall! Don't fall and hurt that pretty face.' But of course I was so excited that I *did* fall, right on my dumb face. Mickey came over because I started bawling my eyes out." Madge shrugged and snorted. "So I guess in the end I got my way."

"We should go back together," Jocelyn suggested lightly. "Maybe next summer. I'll have some money saved up by then. It could be nice to get away."

"I'd like to see it again. This time I won't climb any benches."

They ate at their usual table. Madge stayed silent, forking

down the eggs and porridge on her tray. It seemed to take longer to get their food these days, but Jocelyn didn't mind. Her appetite had improved, but not much. Madge, on the other hand, was hungrier than ever. She had put on a little weight because of it, but she simply looked prettier; Jocelyn was fairly sure nothing at all could take away Madge's appeal.

The orderlies had noticed, of course, David and the others swarming around like vultures whenever Madge flounced down the corridor alone, but she only had eyes for Tanner. And that was generally in her favor, considering he practically drooled on himself whenever she happened by.

"Nurse Ash."

Jocelyn started, dropping her spoon into her oatmeal and splattering her uniform. She hastily dabbed at the mess with her napkin, twisting to find Warden Crawford standing next to her, his hand flattened on the table near her tray. Madge, apparently, had been too engrossed in her scrambled eggs to notice his approach.

"Enjoying a leisurely breakfast, I see." He retracted his hand, digging into his pockets for a mint before clearing his throat and nodding toward the exit. "I need you in my office."

"I'll be done in just a—"

"*Now.*"

Jocelyn paled. He had never used that tone of voice before. She quickly gathered her napkin and drink onto her tray and scurried to the drop-off window. As she returned, Madge gave her a quick, nervous wave. Jocelyn didn't dare return it.

Oh God. Was she in trouble? Following him out of the cafeteria, Jocelyn ran through everything she had done the day before. It was possible she had given someone the wrong medication or the wrong dose, or she might have forgotten to mark down her rounds correctly. But that was so unlikely! She paid excellent attention to detail, even when tired, even when under immense pressure. . . .

"You can relax, Nurse Ash. Nothing is amiss."

"It's just that usually you don't summon me that way, sir. . . ."

Warden Crawford chuckled, nodding and munching on his mint. "Today is unusual. Today is special."

Special? Jocelyn didn't like the way he lingered over that word. They arrived at his office, but they stopped there only briefly. She stood near the door, watching him collect a stack of files from his desk and a leather bag that she knew to carry his medical instruments. Unlike his office, his instruments were kept in perfect order, a fact she observed on the rare occasion he even brought them on his rounds.

They made the descent to the basement, a trip that Jocelyn still found unsettling. It didn't matter how many times she traversed those steps, she never got over the feeling of the wet cold creeping into her bones.

"And how is Nurse Fullerton?" he asked, breezy.

"Oh. Fine, I think. Working hard like the rest of us," Jocelyn answered.

"You don't sound confident."

"I can't see inside her head," she replied.

"More's the pity," Warden Crawford said with a short laugh. "She seemed quite disturbed after treating Mr. Heimline yesterday. I had to calm her down for an hour afterward."

Jocelyn slowed—Madge hadn't told her a single thing about

this. It wasn't like Madge to keep something dramatic from her. "This is the first I'm hearing of it."

"Hm." He shrugged, leading her down the last of the stairs and toward the yawning archway. "She must have made a full recovery then. Forget I said anything."

She wasn't likely to forget, but Jocelyn tried not to dwell on Madge's problems, recognizing that they were on their way yet again to Lucy's room. Normally, Crawford would stop well short of the girl's door, aware that even the briefest glimpse of him could send her into a spiraling panic.

But this time he marched up to the door without a hitch in his step, motioning to two of the orderlies to join him. He stopped and turned to look at Jocelyn, watching her down the thin, arched bridge of his nose. "Why don't you wait for us in Theater Seven, Nurse Ash."

"But Lucy is always so calm when I'm—"

"You will wait in Theater Seven."

Jocelyn snapped her mouth shut, taking a tiny step away in the face of his command. She had the gall to hesitate, but Crawford stared at her until she began to leave, his eyes never straying from her as she continued down the hall. She didn't look away either, glancing over her shoulder to watch as the orderlies opened the rusted, scraping door to Lucy's room.

The door to the operating theater had to be opened, cutting off her view of the corridor. The last sound she heard before stepping inside was a single, piercing shriek.

This was a nightmare. She was paralyzed, in her skin but out of her mind, watching as if her soul had departed and now hovered just above the ground. Why couldn't she move? It was fear, she knew—fear and sharp, crushing failure.

Lucy, God help her, was strapped to the operating table, her cries long since snuffed out by a hateful gag.

Jocelyn's fingernails cut into her palms and her mouth behind her white paper mask had grown clammy. The girl's black, glassy eyes stared up into the light hanging over the table, reflecting the perfect yellow circles. She had gone still. That was worse. When they had first dragged her in, she had kicked and screamed and struggled, but now, facing her wide-eyed resignation, Jocelyn felt she had given up.

He wants to cut it open and scoop out what's inside.

A shiver propelled Jocelyn forward and into the harsh light over the operating table. The orderlies who were there to assist, also garbed in white with their mouths covered by crisp paper, paused with their hands in midair, staring. Warden Crawford stopped what he was doing, too, setting down the gleaming bone saw.

"Your participation in the procedure is not yet required, Nurse Ash," he told her gently. "You may step back."

The room was cold. Too cold. How could he operate with steady hands when it felt like they were all encased in ice? And now, over the paper mask covering half his face, Jocelyn could see just his eyes. Just his eyes, and they were different. Honed. Sharpened like a razor, cutting into her as readily as he was about to cut into little Lucy.

Little Lucy, who still wouldn't speak, but smiled whenever they got to see the birds outside, and smiled a little bigger when Jocelyn called her "sparrow."

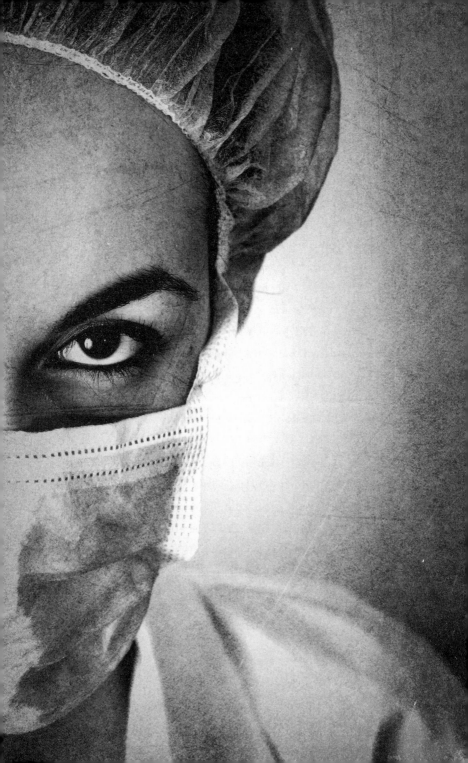

"Is this . . . is this really necessary? She's been improving, sir. Steadily. You've seen it, I know you have. Why would you—"

"You may step back."

Don't let him cut open my head.

"No," Jocelyn said. Her voice shook, but she pushed through it. This was all that mattered. Lucy, and doing right by her, was all that mattered. It was why she had become a nurse. It was why she had even stayed at dark, horrible Brookline in the first place. "No, sir, I can't let you do this. There is no medical justification for this procedure. You know it isn't right. We both know it isn't right."

Warden Crawford rounded on her, exploding at her with a sudden cry that sent her sprawling backward. He ripped off his paper mask, half roaring with outrage. "You *dare* question me? You *dare?*" His entire body shook, his eyes larger, blacker, and sharper than she had ever seen them. He looked down, noticing the pronounced tremor in his arms. "Stupid girl. Now nothing can be done today." He grunted again and waved vaguely at the orderlies. "Clean up. Get her out of here."

One of the orderlies cleared his throat, shuffling. "But sir, the electroconvulsive shock—"

The warden spun and slammed his hands against the instrument tray, sending gleaming steel in every direction, the sound jarring them all. *"Does anyone in this fucking building listen to me anymore?"*

Jocelyn stared, sucking in breaths so hard her paper mask sank in and out against her mouth, expanding and deflating like bellows. His voice rang in the small operating theater, the orderlies stunned into similar silences.

"You," he finally said, collecting his breath and pointing at her. "Out. And you two, help me get this patient back to confinement."

✗ ✗ ✗ ✗ ✗

"You didn't tell me about what happened with Dennis Heimline." Jocelyn didn't mean for it to come out so coldly, but she needed to discuss something—*anything*—to get her mind off what she had seen in Theater 7. He was going to operate. On Lucy. He was going to operate on Lucy and it was completely unnecessary.

Lucy was right. Why does he want to perform surgery on her so badly?

Madge paced outside the back stoop of Brookline. It was one of the few places nurses could find some privacy. And it was one of the few places Madge could sneak a cigarette without a lecture from Nurse Kramer. Jocelyn hated how much her friend was smoking, but she envied Madge the release of a vice. Maybe she ought to take up one of her own.

"He just . . . He snapped at me." Madge paused, looking out over the distant town. Camford crowded up to the hill where Brookline and the rest of the college sat. It was odd, Jocelyn thought, to even consider the collegiate life going on around them. The students avoided Brookline as if it were contagious. She was beginning to understand why.

"He was talking about the White Mountains again," Madge added, regarding the burning-cherry end of her cigarette. "And then something just changed and he wasn't himself. Dennis is odd but harmless. He's never threatened me, never said anything to frighten me at all. I don't know what happened. . . .

One minute it was White Mountains this, White Mountains that, and then he lunged for me. He grabbed me around the throat, Joss! It was horrible." She shivered, taking another long drag. "*I want to pose you*. That's what he said. God, it was just so, so horrible. *I want to pose you, you would be so beautiful*."

"Why didn't you tell me this?" Jocelyn asked softly. She sat on the stoop, hiding from the drizzle under a shallow, shingled overhang.

"You've been so wrapped up with Lucy. . . . I didn't want to worry you."

"Yeah, well, you won't have to think about that anymore." Jocelyn pinched the bridge of her nose, sighing. She had *had* to intervene, but now who would protect Lucy from the warden? "I really stuffed it up, Madge. I'll probably get fired *and* I'll never work with Lucy again."

Her friend flicked away the cigarette, aiming it at a damp tree trunk. They sat together on the stoop, Madge with her arm flung over Jocelyn's shoulders. "For what it's worth, I think you did the right thing. Anyway, I heard Kramer buzzing to one of the other girls. It sounds like Crawford wants you to work with a new patient coming in. You might not be able to help Lucy, but maybe this one will be easier."

Jocelyn nodded, swallowing her cynical retort.

"Well, lovely, I'm off," Madge said, leaning over to squeeze Jocelyn in a one-armed hug. She stood and brushed off her rain-flecked uniform. "Crawford wants to see me. Again. I think the gross old fart has a crush on me or something."

"What does he want to see you about?" Jocelyn asked quickly. She couldn't explain her sudden sense of dread.

"Something about Dennis. He says I have to see 'it' now, what-ever that means," Madge said, sounding sad. Resigned. "He says I have to see how far gone Dennis is, that there's no hope for him. When there's no hope, he says, there's only survival. You know"—she paused with the door open, her full lips swishing to the side—"I think I really will dye my hair dark. I could look like Jackie, right? Maybe I'll feel better with a little more glamour in my life. I'll see what Tanner thinks. We've got another date tonight. I bet this time we'll really go all the way."

"*Ash*. Nurse Ash. Huh. That's a fittingly macabre name for this charming little dungeon."

Jocelyn blinked at the new patient, taking stock of his slim, tall form, his carelessly tossed black hair and almost unnaturally green eyes. If he were one of the orderlies, he would immedi-ately be on Madge's short list for seduction. Even Jocelyn had to admit, in a quiet, shameful way, that she found him incredibly pretty. Pretty, because there was something fluid and feminine about his frame and his hands, and the way he leaned against the white, spare bed, his arms over his chest, his legs crossed at the ankles.

"I won't fuss if it helps you to have a sense of humor about all this," Jocelyn said blithely. "We're going to have to get to know each other," she added, consulting the detailed history in front of her. That was nice, at least, to know a single thing about this person, unlike the strangely vacant past of Lucy. Of Dennis. "And I prefer my patients cheerful, if at all possible. Coopera-tive, at the very least."

"Aye, aye," he murmured, saluting. His lips resolved into a

smirk, their natural resting position. "And how do you run the Good Ship Loony Bin. Is it a *tight* ship or a loose one?"

He wagged his eyebrows, but it was not nearly enough to unseat her. Old Mr. Goldblatt in room sixteen would flirt outrageously, using sexual terminology and phrases that not even Madge could decipher.

"I know this must be difficult for you," she began, glancing at his chart again and at the reason for admittance. This was a new one. Luckily, her only job was to administer whatever medicines the doctors prescribed and check in on him occasionally. It wasn't her job to cure him. And maybe that was for the best, as she clearly wasn't curing much of anything lately.

DESMOND, CARRICK ANDREW

SEX: MALE

REASON FOR ADMITTANCE: UNNATURAL SEXUAL PREDILECTIONS

Well, that covered a wide swath.

He must have noticed her eyes widening as he quickly laughed and said, "Got caught in bed with the neighbor boy. Well, young man, really. I'm not *that* much of a pervert."

"I don't believe you're a pervert at all, Mr. Desmond," she replied, just as readily. She looked up briskly from the file, meeting his bright, challenging stare. "I don't like words like that. They don't do anything but shame. Treatment is not about shame."

His thick brows went up, up, up in surprise. He looked at her as if he could see all the way into her mind. "You shock me, Nurse Ash. But in the very best of ways."

She smirked, accustomed to the flirtation of patients eager to get on her good side and slip the rules. "Please let me know if you have any trouble settling in. Accommodating to life here can be"—Awful. *Impossible*—"Tricky."

"Oh, trust me, nothing I can't handle. I was born to jailors."

Jocelyn took a few steps backward toward the door, grimacing. "I'm afraid life must have been very unfair for you."

His eyes, green and light, fixed on her again through his fall of dark hair. "I'm afraid it's very unfair for everyone. You might not think I'm a pervert, but unfortunately, you're not the one in power here. You're not the one with the keys."

"I'll check in with you again shortly," she said, leaving before he could tempt her to stay another moment.

The door clicked shut behind her and locked, and not a second afterward came the scream. She knew that scream. It had driven her from sleep and stayed in her nightmares ever since.

Lucy.

No, she thought, racing down the hall. *Don't let him cut her open.*

CHAPTER
№ 8

$\mathcal{S}$he was too late, of course. She had known that would be the case even as she sped down the corridor, almost smashing into Nurse Kramer, who had positioned herself like a sentry at the top of the stairs leading to the basement.

"Nobody is allowed below right now," she said sternly, putting out her arms like a first baseman to keep Jocelyn from forcing her way through. "Nobody."

"I need to see Lucy. She's screaming."

"Other nurses are with her." Nurse Kramer's mouth clamped shut, her fleshy face jiggling to a standstill. "You're not needed."

"What other nurses? I should be with her."

"Nurse Fullerton, for one. Just calm down, Ash, and get back to work. I don't want to see you in this hallway for the rest of the afternoon, do you understand me?"

Lucy screamed again, this time harder, a raw, helpless sound that pierced straight through to Jocelyn's spine. *No, no, no.* She was supposed to protect her. She was supposed to make sure nothing worse happened to that child.

"I need you to say that you understand me, Nurse Ash."

Jocelyn threw up her hands, stalking away. "I understand. I *understand*, if that's even possible in this godforsaken place."

She rounded the corner and disappeared into the nurses'

station. Maybe if she waited long enough, Nurse Kramer would need to leave for a toilet break and give Jocelyn an opening. But by then it would be too late. Far too late. Still. She tidied until there was no more tidying to do. She took prescriptions and handed out doses in the dispensary. She even paced up and down the hall. All the while, she stayed as close to the stairwell as possible, but Kramer refused to budge.

By five o'clock the screams had stopped, and Jocelyn could only wonder what they had done to Lucy.

I'm sorry, little sparrow.

Her fury turned to Warden Crawford, and then it turned just as swiftly to Madge. How could she be a part of this? Hadn't she been just as doting on Lucy? Lobotomies were an absolute last resort. Surgeries of *any* kind were a last resort. And even if it came to a lobotomy, there were easier, more modern methods that absolutely did not involve a bone saw. Whatever was going on in the basement, she had to put an end to it.

But all Jocelyn could do was wait. She watched the nurses come and go for supper. No sign of Madge. Didn't she have a date? It wasn't like Madge to miss something like that, not when she couldn't shut up about Tanner and his *gorgeous* blue eyes for fifteen seconds.

But the hours blurred together, and between skipping lunch, supper, and all the usual coffee breaks in between, Jocelyn was worn down. She was *exhausted*. Sleep snuck up on her, the after-hours low halogen glow of the lobby lulling her into a doze she hadn't wanted or expected. There were no dreams and little rest, just darkness and the hard, sudden slide into unconsciousness.

And then there was giggling.

It was soft at first, distant, and for a fuzzy, sleepy moment Jocelyn thought she had finally begun to dream. But the laughter continued, louder, sharper. Not laughter. Giggling. Madge's giggling. Jocelyn's head flew up, a string of drool snapping between her lower lip and her forearm. She had curled up against the dispensary counter, her knees tucked up on the second rung of the stool. Now she rubbed her eyes, her face, working blood flow and sense back into her body.

The giggling came again, a feminine, flirty sound that wound up from the depths of Brookline. There were voices, too, but they were muffled and unintelligible at this extreme distance. Jocelyn tumbled off the stool and pulled off her heels—she could run better in bare stockings—and raced to the stairs. Nurse Kramer was of course long gone, having left for dinner and then sleep. A few orderlies and nurses were circulating on the lobby level, but they didn't seem to notice Jocelyn stumbling toward the stairs.

Again she plunged into the cold and again she fought off the creeping dread that seeped over her like a sticky, oozing tar. She abandoned her hard-soled shoes on one of the lower steps, shuffling with free hands and quiet feet to the archway and the soft, winding giggles that came from within.

Now the voices were louder, stronger, and Jocelyn began to make out the words. There were no orderlies to stop her as she stepped beneath the dark arch marking off the corridor.

"W-wait . . . What are you doing? Madge? *What are you doing?*"

Tanner. She could hear the panic in his voice, the high tremor that made him sound like a frightened little boy. Jocelyn ran faster, trying not to slide and fall on her sweaty, stockinged

feet. Where *were* they? She panted, out of breath, ignoring how the corridor became darker and darker, closing in, the corridor more like a tunnel that focused to just a miniscule barrel of light. But she jolted to a stop as the sudden cry of the other patients went up, as if in solidarity with Madge's laughter. A refrain of wild, terrible sympathy.

And then it was a chant. She couldn't hear Lucy's screams but she could hear the others, Dennis and his ilk, their cries coalescing into the same phrase she had heard on that first awful night.

"Help her, help her, HELP HER!"

She found them in Theater 7.

Jocelyn leaped for the doorframe, anchoring her slick and unreliable feet by hoisting herself into the room. She didn't want to freeze. It was the worst possible moment to freeze. Yet she couldn't move. Madge was there, standing on the same operating table where they had bound and gagged Lucy. Below, arms out as if to catch her from a sudden fall, Tanner eased back and forth, eyes glued to Madge, who was swaying on the wheeled table.

"Careful, doll," she giggled. In her right hand she held a sleek, stainless steel hammer, the kind used with an orbitoclast for lobotomies. "You'll fall! Don't fall and hurt that pretty face."

"Let me get you down from there," Tanner was saying, licking his lips nervously and trying to ease toward her. But Madge reeled at his slightest movement, the table shaking, threatening to spill her onto the floor. She swung the hammer, first at him and then at the open air before her.

"Why don't you just come down?" he pleaded. Sweat glistened

on his forehead. The chanting grew louder, earsplitting, and gathering in speed. Jocelyn inched carefully into the room, hands up in surrender.

"I saw him," Madge was saying. She sounded scared. Little. "I saw Mickey Mouse, but where was Minnie? She wasn't there. And she's so, so pretty. So pretty. But now she's cracked. Now she's broken."

Jocelyn had nearly reached the pool of light cast by the operating bulbs, but Madge didn't notice, swaying precariously on the gurney, her arms high in the air, hammer swinging like a pendulum.

"Just come down from there and we can talk," Tanner coaxed, still prepared to catch her if she fell, which was looking more and more likely.

Jocelyn wondered if she could somehow climb up onto the table and tackle Madge, bring her down gently while also disarming her. But that seemed like far too much to attempt without either both of them hitting the ground from a height or Madge accidentally smashing her with the hammer.

"But he said I would see!" Madge shrieked. Her scream only drove the chanting higher, louder, and the words thumped at the base of Jocelyn's skull.

"Help her, help her!"

"Careful, doll," Madge breathed, laughing, giggling, her voice hiccupping into hysterics. "Careful, doll! Careful! You'll fall! Don't fall and hurt that pretty face!"

Jocelyn saw the hammer go up with more purpose this time, *Freeman* stamped into the shining steel. Both she and Tanner leapt for the table too late. Madge caught herself on the

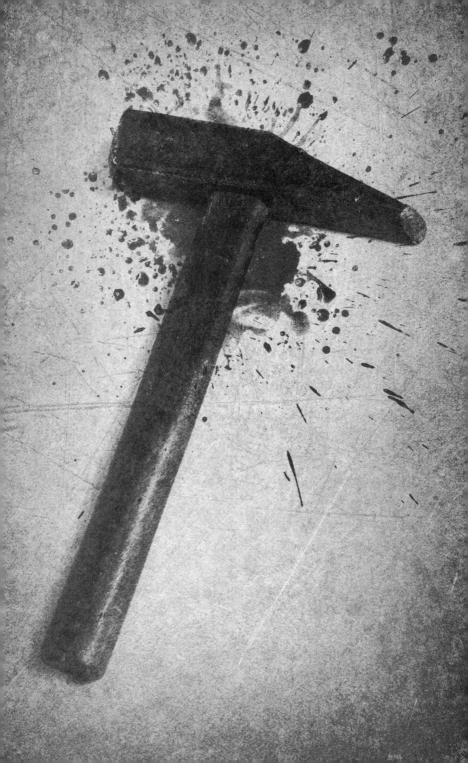

upswing, rocketing the hammer into her mouth. Teeth shattered, tiny bits of white falling on them like a shower of sand. Jocelyn tossed up her hands, screaming, watching through the splay of her fingers as the hammer landed again, this time dead center of Madge's forehead.

She was still giggling, giggling, giggling. *Smash.*

Tanner grabbed her by the ankles, pulling her down to the floor as best he could, dodging the hammer blows that rained down indiscriminately. While he brought her to the ground, Jocelyn tried to reach for the hammer, but Madge struggled, her giggles turning into shrill arpeggio of screams. She dodged and bucked and smashed the hammer into her forehead again and again, until Jocelyn took a blow to the shoulder herself, finally wrestling the thing out of her grasp.

The hammer had broken the skin, and the deep, dark bruising spread like spidery shadows from the middle of Madge's forehead. The blood ran over them all as Jocelyn and Tanner pinned her arms, held her, her laughter dying down as the light seeped out of her eyes.

"M-Madge, Madge, can you breathe? Oh God, can you breathe? Just stay with me, I'll get someone. . . . I'll get help. I'll get you help." Jocelyn tore a strip of cotton from her uniform, trying to mop up the free-flowing blood and stop the bleeding at its epicenter.

But the blood poured down Madge's face, splitting over her nose and into her mouth, onto Jocelyn, dripping onto the floor, so red it looked black. "I fell and hurt my pretty face," she mumbled, words jumbled from her broken and missing teeth. "I guess he got his way."

"Hold on, Madge, I know it's bad, just . . . Please hold on."

"Why," Tanner whispered. Again and again. "Why? *Why?*"

A shadow fell over them, swallowing up the meager yellow light of the operating lamps. Madge had gone limp in their arms and the shrieks of the patients, at last, had ebbed. Jocelyn felt a heavy hand fall on her shoulder. The warden's.

She shivered and tried to cast off his grip.

"Surely you see now, Nurse Ash," he said. "Sometimes there really is no hope. What could you have done? What could any of us have done? If we hadn't put Lucy's mind at ease—if we had not given her a peace she could not give herself—she might have done this same awful thing to herself. Dennis . . . Dennis could slip away from us any day now."

"I don't . . . Madge didn't do this to herself." Jocelyn couldn't look down. She couldn't look into her friend's broken face. Her skin was so cold, they were both so cold, the blood and the sudden gush of tears felt all the hotter. Stinging. "She didn't do this. There was nothing wrong with her. *I know there was nothing wrong with her.*"

She heard footsteps and glanced to the side, watching as two male orderlies filed into Theater 7.

"Escort Mr. Frye to his room, please," Warden Crawford said, tut-tutting at Tanner and squeezing Jocelyn's shoulder so hard she could feel the bones give and crack.

"I'd like him to stay," Jocelyn whispered. "Madge . . . She really cared for him."

"It's best that he go."

He wasn't given a choice in the matter. They caught eyes, she and Tanner, as the orderlies hauled him away from Madge, his spectacles askew, his mouth open to call for help. But then the door shut and she was alone with the warden, Madge limp and lifeless in her arms.

"She was going to dye her hair like Jackie Kennedy," Jocelyn murmured, wiping a stained piece of blond hair off of Madge's cheek. "She wanted to be glamorous."

"That's nice."

"You don't care," she growled. "You don't care about Lucy. You don't care about me or about Madge. You don't care about anything."

"Now, that's not true," he said warmly, gently, shifting so that he could crouch in front of her and face her. He reached out, and she tensed as his hand cupped her chin, forcing her to meet his cold, steady gaze. "I care about the future. I care about making sure things like this never happen again—it's senseless, useless."

Jocelyn couldn't argue with that, but she couldn't look at him anymore, either. *I couldn't help her.* That was the only thought filling her head. *I couldn't help her.*

She hadn't helped Lucy, and she certainly hadn't helped Madge. What kind of nurse was she? What kind of *person* was she?

"Hush," Warden Crawford said. She hadn't even realized she was crying. The smile he gave her was gentle, fatherly, and for a brief, terrible moment his presence didn't fill her with unease. "Some patients are beyond help," he told her, lifting Madge carefully from her grasp, "but they are not beyond *use*. We will learn from this, Nurse Ash. Trust me, in time you will learn."

Brookline's twisted legacy runs long and deep, and Cal, Oliver, and Jocelyn are only part of the story.

Keep reading for sneak peeks at *Asylum*, *Sanctum*, and *Catacomb*, and find out how the stories intertwine. . . .

PROLOGUE

They built it out of stone—dark gray stone, pried loose from the unforgiving mountains. It was a house for those who could not take care of themselves, for those who heard voices, who had strange thoughts and did strange things. The house was meant to keep them in. Once they came, they never left.

CHAPTER
№ 1

*D*an felt like he was going to be sick.

The narrow, gravelly road had been jostling his cab for at least five miles now, and that was on top of his first-day jitters. His driver kept cursing about dents and flat tires. Dan just hoped he wouldn't be expected to pay for any damage—the trip from the airport was already expensive enough.

Although it was early afternoon, the light outside was dim thanks to the dense forest on either side of the road. *It would be easy to get lost in those woods*, Dan thought.

"Still alive back there?"

"What? Yeah, I'm fine," Dan said, realizing he hadn't spoken since he'd gotten in the car. "Just ready for some even ground is all."

Finally, the cab came to a break in the trees and everything turned dappled and silvery green in the summer sunshine.

There it was: New Hampshire College. The place Dan would be spending the next five weeks.

This summer school—Dan's lifeline—had been the proverbial light at the end of the tunnel all school year long. He'd be hanging out with kids who wanted to learn, who actually did their homework beforehand and not up against their lockers in a messy dash before the bell. He couldn't wait to be there already.

Out the window, Dan saw buildings that he recognized from the college's website. They were charming brick colonials placed around a quad with emerald-green grass, perfectly cut and trimmed. These were the academic buildings, Dan knew, where he would be taking classes. Already a few early birds were out on the lawn tossing a Frisbee back and forth. How had those guys made friends so fast? Maybe it really would be that easy here.

The driver hesitated at a four-way stop; diagonally to the right stood a pretty, down-home church with a tall white steeple, then a row of houses stretching beyond. Craning forward out of his seat, Dan saw the cabbie flick on his right turn signal.

"It's left, actually," Dan blurted, sinking back down in his seat.

The driver shrugged. "If you say so. Damn machine can't seem to make up its mind." As if to illustrate, the cabbie banged his fist on the GPS display bolted to the center of the dash. It looked like the path it had mapped out for them ended here.

"It's left," Dan repeated, less confident this time. He wasn't actually sure how he knew the way—he hadn't looked up directions ahead of time—but there was something about that pristine little church that stirred a memory, and if not a memory, a gut instinct.

Dan drummed his fingers on the seat, impatient to see where he would be living. The regular dorms were being renovated over the summer, so all the College Prep students were being housed in an older building called Brookline, which his admissions packet had called a "retired mental health facility and historical site." In other words, an *asylum*.

At the time, Dan had been surprised to find there were no pictures of Brookline up on the website. But he understood why when the cab rounded a corner and there it was.

It didn't matter that the college had slapped a fresh coat of paint on the outer walls, or that some enterprising gardener had gone a little overboard planting cheerful hydrangea bushes along the path—Brookline loomed at the far end of the road like a warning. Dan had never imagined that a building could look *threatening*, but Brookline managed that feat and then some. It actually seemed to be watching him.

Turn around now, whispered the voice in his head.

Dan shivered, unable to stop himself from imagining how patients in the old days felt when they were checked into the asylum. Did they know? Did some of them have this same weird feeling of panic, or were they too far gone to understand?

Then he shook his head. These were ridiculous thoughts. . . . He was a student, not a patient. And as he'd assured Paul and Sandy, Brookline was no longer an asylum; it had closed its doors in 1972 when the college purchased it to make a functional dorm with co-ed floors and communal bathrooms.

"Okay, this is it," said the cab driver, although Dan noticed he'd stopped about thirty feet shy of the curb. Maybe Dan wasn't the only one who got weird vibes from this place. Still, he reached into his wallet and forked over three of the twenties his parents had given him.

"Keep the change," he said, climbing out.

Something about rolling up his sleeves and grabbing his stuff from the trunk finally made the day feel real in Dan's mind. A guy in a blue baseball cap wandered by, a stack of worn comic books in his arms. That made Dan smile. *My people*, he thought. He walked into the dorm. For the next five weeks, this was home.

CHAPTER
№ 2

*I*f a new BMW in the school parking lot gave you clout at Dan's high school, then Apple products and sheer volume of books seemed to grant the cool factor at NHCP.

That's what they were supposed to call the program, as Dan quickly learned. The college student volunteers who were there to hand out room keys and help kids move in kept saying, "Welcome to *NHCP*!" and the one time Dan actually called it "New Hampshire College Prep," they gave him a look like he was sweet but simple.

Dan walked up the front steps and found himself in a large entrance hall. The enormous chandelier couldn't overcome the darkness caused by all the wood paneling and overstuffed furniture. Through a grand archway across from the entrance, Dan spotted a wide staircase, and halls leading in on either side. Even the students bustling in and out did nothing to dispel the feeling of heaviness.

Dan started up the stairs with his suitcases. Three long flights later, he arrived at his room, number 3808. Dan put down his bags and opened the door, only to discover that his assigned roommate had already moved in. Or maybe *filed* in would be more accurate. Books, manga magazines, almanacs of all shapes and sizes (most tending toward biology) lay in neat, color-coordinated order on the provided bookshelves. His roommate had taken up exactly half of the space in the room, with his suitcases zipped up and tucked neatly under the closer bed. Half of the closet was already filled with shirts, slacks, and coats on hangers—white hangers for shirts and jackets, blue for pants.

It looked like the guy had been living here for weeks.

Dan hauled his suitcases onto the unclaimed bed, then checked over the furniture that was his for the summer. The bed, bedside table, and desk all seemed to be in good condition. He opened the top desk drawer out of idle curiosity, wondering if he would find a Gideons Bible or maybe a welcome letter. Instead, he discovered a small slip of what looked like film paper. It was old, faded to the point of being almost completely bleached out. Faintly, he could see a man staring up at him, an older, bespectacled gentleman in a doctor's coat and dark shirt. Nothing about the photo was all that remarkable, except for the eyes—or to be more accurate, where the eyes had been. Messily— or perhaps angrily—someone had scratched them out.

SANCTUM

PROLOGUE

*I*t was a fantasy of lights and sounds and smells, crooked candy-striped tents, and laughter that burst like cannon fire out of the winding paths. Curiosities lurked around every corner. A man belched flames from a podium. The scent of fried cakes and popcorn hung sweet and heavy on the air, tantalizing until it became sickening. And in the very last tent was a man with a long beard—a man who didn't promise riches or oddities or even a glimpse into the future. No. The man in the last tent promised the one thing the little boy wanted most of all.

Control.

CHAPTER

1

You guys are not even going to believe this, Dan typed, shaking his head at the computer screen. *A "memory manipulation expert"? Is that even a real thing? Anyway, just watch the video, and let me know what you think!*

His cursor hovered over that last line—it sounded so desperate. But whatever, Dan was starting to get desperate here. His last three messages had gone unanswered, and he wasn't even sure if Abby and Jordan were still reading them.

He hit send.

Dan leaned away from his laptop, rolling his neck and listening to the soft pops of his spine adjusting. Then he closed the thing—maybe a little too sharply—and stood up, shoving the computer into his book bag between loose papers and folders. The bell rang just as he finished packing, and he filed out of the library into the hall.

The students in the wide corridor surged forward in one long column. Dan spotted a few kids from his third-period calculus class, and they waved at him as he approached their bank of lockers. Missy, a short brunette with freckles splattered across her nose, had decorated the door of her locker with just about every *Doctor Who* sticker and postcard she could get her hands on. A tall, gangly boy named Tariq was grabbing books from the locker next to hers, and beside him stood the shortest guy in twelfth grade, Beckett.

"Hey, Dan," Missy greeted him. "We missed you at lunch. Where'd you run off to?"

"Oh, I was in the library," Dan said. "I just had to finish something for AP Lit."

"Man, you guys have to do so much work for that class," Beckett said. "I'm glad I stuck with regular English."

"So, Dan, we were just talking about *Macbeth* when you walked up. Were you planning on going?"

"Yeah, I heard the set is amazing," Tariq said, shutting his locker with a clang.

"I didn't even know we were doing *Macbeth*," Dan said. "Is it like a drama club thing?"

"Yes, and Annie Si is in it. That's reason enough to go right there." Beckett shot the boys a mischievous smile, one Dan only barely returned, and then the group started down the hallway. Dan couldn't remember what classes the rest of them had next, but even if he hadn't been doing any work in the library, he really was headed to the second floor for AP Lit. It wasn't his favorite class, but Abby had read most of the books on the syllabus and had promised to give him a rundown at some point, which made it better.

"We should check it out," Tariq said. He was wearing a sweater three times too big for him and skinny pants. It made him look a little like a bobblehead. "And, Dan, you should join us. I might be able to get us free tickets. I know the lead techie."

"I don't know, I've never really liked *Macbeth*. It hits too close to home for OCD people like me," Dan deadpanned, rubbing furiously at an invisible stain on his sleeve.

Both Missy and Tariq stared back at him blankly.

"You know?" He chuckled weakly. " 'Out, damned spot'?"

"Oh, is that from the play?" Tariq asked.

"Yeah, it's . . . It's like one of the most famous lines." He frowned. Abby and Jordan would've gotten it. Didn't everyone have to read *Macbeth* for school? "Anyway, I'll see you guys later."

Dan peeled off from the group and headed upstairs. He pulled out his phone and sent off a quick text to both Jordan and Abby: "Nobody here gets my sense of humor. Help!" Twenty minutes later, when he was sitting bored in class, Jordan still hadn't texted back and Abby had sent a lukewarm "LOL."

What was wrong? Where had his friends *gone*? It wasn't like they were that busy. . . . Just last week, Jordan had been telling him on Facebook chat how insanely tedious his classes were. Nothing was challenging, he'd said, after the classes at the New Hampshire College Prep program. Dan sympathized, but honestly, the classes were the last thing he remembered from their summer in New Hampshire. What he couldn't stop thinking about was what had happened in their dorm, Brookline—formerly an insane asylum run by a twisted warden, Daniel Crawford.

When he wasn't thinking about *that* small detail, though, he was thinking about Jordan and Abby. When they'd first returned from the college campus, he'd gotten texts and emails from them constantly, but now they hardly talked. Missy, Tariq, and Beckett were okay, he supposed, but Jordan and Abby were different. Jordan knew how to push his buttons, but it was always good-natured and made the three of them laugh. And if

Jordan pushed a little too hard, Abby was there to call him out and restore the balance. Really, she was the linchpin that held their group together—a group that in Dan's mind seemed worth keeping up.

So why were his friends ignoring him?

Dan glanced at the clock, groaning. Two more hours until the end of the day. Two more hours until he could dash home and get online to see if his friends wanted to chat.

He sighed and scooted down into his seat, reluctantly putting his phone away.

Strange to think that a place as dangerous as Brookline had brought them together, and normal life was pulling them apart.

✗ ✗ ✗ ✗ ✗

A half-eaten peanut butter sandwich sat on the plate next to his laptop. At his feet, his AP History textbook collected leaves. The crisp fall air normally helped him focus, but instead of doing homework, like he really ought to, he was busy going through the file he had made about Brookline. After the prep program ended, Dan had made sure to organize the notes he'd made, the research he'd done, and the photographs he'd collected, and turn it into one neat file.

He found himself returning to browse through it more than he should. Even with all these original documents, so much of the warden's history was still missing. And after learning that he might actually be related to the warden through his birth parents—that this horrible man might be his great-uncle and even his namesake—Dan felt like this was a hole in his personal history, a mystery that he very much needed to solve.

At the moment, though, the file was just a distracting way to pass the time while he waited for Jordan and Abby to log on. What was that phrase his dad always liked to use? *Hurry up and wait. . . .*

"Could I be any more pathetic?" Dan muttered, pushing both hands into his dark, messy hair.

"I think you're just fine, sweetheart."

Right. Better to keep the gloomy asides silent in the future. Dan looked up to see his mom, Sandy, standing on the porch, smiling at him. She was holding a steaming cup of cocoa, one he hoped was for him.

"Hard at work?" she asked, nodding to the forgotten textbook on the floor at his feet.

"I'm almost done," he replied with a shrug, taking the cocoa from her with cupped hands, his sweater sleeves pulled over his fingers. "I think I'm allowed a break every once in a while."

"True," Sandy said, offering him an apologetic half smile. "It's just . . . well, a few months ago, you seemed so excited about applying early decision to Penn, but here we are in October and that deadline's coming up fast."

"I've got plenty of time," Dan said unconvincingly.

"Maybe for the essay, but don't you think the admissions people will find it odd that you stopped doing all your extracurriculars your senior year? Couldn't you get an internship? Even if it was just one day on the weekends, I think it would make a big difference. And maybe you should visit some other campuses, too—you know, early decision isn't the best choice for everyone."

"I don't need more extracurriculars as long as I keep my four point oh. And besides, NHCP will look great on my apps."

Sandy's pale brow furrowed, a chilly wind ruffling her shoulder-length hair as she looked away from him, staring out at the trees surrounding the porch. She hugged herself and shook her head. This was how she always reacted when NHCP came up; unlike Jordan and Abby, who had been able to spin and massage the truth for their parents when it came to Brookline, Dan's parents more or less knew the whole story. They had been there when the police questioned Dan; they had listened as he recounted being attacked, pinned to the ground. . . . Just mentioning that place in their presence was like whispering a curse.

"But sure," Dan said, blowing on the hot chocolate, "I could look for an internship or something. No sweat."

Sandy's face relaxed and her arms dropped to her sides. "Would you? That would really be amazing, kiddo."

Dan nodded, going so far as to open a new browser window on his laptop and Google something. He typed in "zookeeper internship" and tilted the laptop slightly away from her.

"Thanks for the cocoa," he added.

"Of course." She ruffled his hair, and Dan breathed a sigh of relief. "You haven't gone out much lately. Doesn't Missy have a birthday coming up soon? I remember you going to her party around Halloween last year."

"Probably," he said with a shrug.

"Or your other . . . your other friends?" She stumbled over the word *friends*. "Abby, was it? And the boy?"

She always did that, asking about Abby as if she didn't

remember exactly what her name was. It was like she couldn't believe or accept that he had actually gotten a sort-of girlfriend. To be fair, Dan could hardly believe it sometimes himself.

"Yeah," he said with a noncommittal grunt. "They're busy, though, you know . . . school and work and stuff."

Dynamite job, Dan. Your Oscar's in the mail.

"Work? So *they* have jobs?"

"Subtle, Mom," he muttered. "I can take the hint. . . ."

"I'm sure you can, sweetheart. Oh, before I forget—the mail came. There was something in there for you. . . ."

That was unusual. He never got snail mail. Sandy flicked through the various envelopes that had been tucked in her jacket pocket before dropping one in his lap. The letter looked like it had gotten run through a washing machine and then dragged through the dirt. Dan checked the return address and a cold pain shot through his stomach.

Sandy hovered.

"It's probably junk mail," Dan said lightly, tossing the envelope onto his books. She took the hint, giving him a thin-lipped smile before turning away. He hardly heard the door close as Sandy disappeared back into the house. Dan scrambled for the letter.

Lydia & Newton Sheridan

Sheridan? As in Felix Sheridan? As in his former roommate, the one who had tried to kill him over the summer, either because he went crazy or because he was, what, possessed? When

he closed his eyes Dan could still see Felix's maniacal grin. Possessed or not, Felix had absolutely believed he was the Sculptor reincarnated.

Dan's hands shook as he tore open the envelope. Maybe it was just an apology, he thought—it was entirely possible that Felix's parents wanted to reach out to him and say they were sorry for all the trouble their son had caused him.

Dan drew in a deep breath and double-checked to make sure he was alone. Through the half-open window he could hear Sandy washing the dishes in the kitchen.

Dear Daniel,

You're probably surprised to hear from me, and I'd hoped to avoid sending this letter, but it's become clear that this is the only option.

I really have no right to ask this of you, but please give me a call as soon as you receive this letter. If you don't get in touch . . . Well, I can't say I would blame you.

603-555-2212

Please call.

Regards,

Lydia Sheridan

CHAPTER

2

$\mathcal{D}$an couldn't decide whether to chuck the letter in the garbage or dial the number right away. Inside, he could still hear the quiet clinking of his mother washing and drying the dishes. He read the letter over again, tapping the paper against his knuckles as he weighed his options.

On the one hand, he would be perfectly happy to forget Felix altogether. On the other . . .

On the other hand, it would be a lie to say that he wasn't curious about his old roomie's condition. They had left everything so unresolved. The cold sensation in his stomach refused to go away.

Felix probably needs your help. You needed help, too. Is it really fair to say that anyone is a lost cause?

He looked to the window on his right. His mother was humming now, and the music of it drifted softly out to where he was sitting. A few leaves floated down from the maple tree that lorded over the porch. No matter how many times Paul cut back the branches on it, it kept reaching for the house. But that didn't stop his dad from trying.

Dan picked up his mobile and dialed Lydia Sheridan's number before he could think of an excuse not to.

It rang and rang, and for a moment he was certain she wouldn't pick up. He almost hoped she wouldn't.

"Hello?"

"Hi, Lydia? I mean, Mrs. Sheridan?" His own voice sounded high and strange to his ears.

"That's me. . . . Who is this? I don't recognize the number."

She had Felix's same soft-spoken manner, but hers was a more relaxed and more feminine version of the voice he could still recall.

"This is Dan Crawford. You sent me a letter asking to get in touch. So . . . Well, I'm getting in touch."

The line went quiet for what felt like a lifetime. Finally, he could hear Felix's mother drawing in ragged breaths on the other end.

"Thank you," she said, sounding like she was on the edge of tears. "We're just . . . We don't know what to do anymore. It seemed like he was getting better. The doctors treating him really thought he was improving. But now it's like he's hit a wall. All he does is ask for you, day in and day out—Daniel Crawford, Daniel Crawford."

This news was more than a little unnerving.

"I'm sorry to hear that, but I'm not sure what you want me to do about it," Dan said. Maybe that was cold, but what was he supposed to do? He wasn't a doctor. "It'll probably pass. I bet it will just take time."

"What about for you?" Lydia demanded.

Dan jerked his head back, startled by the sudden chill in her voice.

"Has it passed?" She sighed. "I'm sorry. I'm . . . I'm not sleeping. I'm just so worried about him. I really hate asking this of you . . ."

"But?" Dan prompted. He didn't need to. He saw the question coming from a mile away.

"If you could just go to Morthwaite. See him. See . . . I don't know. I'm begging at this point, do you understand? Begging. I just want him to get better. I just want this to be over." Dan could hear the tears cracking through in her voice again. "It's not over for him, Dan. Is it over for you?"

He had to laugh. Did it feel over? No, not by a long shot. The dreams persisted, as terrifying as ever, often featuring the warden himself. It *wasn't* over, and as twisted as he knew it was, Dan felt a little relieved to hear that he wasn't the only one for whom that was true.

"This might not work," Dan said slowly. "It could make him worse. You realize that, right?" *I don't want that on my head. I can't have that on my head.*

He felt guilty enough for having dragged Abby and Jordan into the mess at Brookline. At least with Felix, he'd been able to tell himself that he was blameless—that that two-faced Professor Reyes had all but admitted to luring Felix down to the basement, where his mind—well, where his mind had *stayed*, is what it sounded like.

"But you'll go?" Mrs. Sheridan sounded so happy. So hopeful. "Oh, thank you, please, I just . . . Thank you."

"So where exactly am I going?" Dan asked, his stomach still one giant knot of dull fear. "And how am I getting there?"

Prologue

*T*hese were the rules as they were first put down:

First, that the Artist should choose an Object dear to the deceased.

Second, that the Artist feel neither guilt nor remorse in the taking.

Third, and most important, that the Object would not hold power until blooded. And that the more innocent the blood for the blooding, the more powerful the result.

Chapter 1

*A*t first the idea of a cross-country road trip had been hard to stomach. If sleeping in a tent wasn't horrible enough, Dan had felt anxious, almost sick, at the prospect of being away from his computer, his books, his *alone time* for two whole weeks. But that was the deal Jordan offered when he wrote to them with the big news: he was moving to New Orleans to live with his uncle.

Perfect chance, his email had said, *to have some time together. You two nerds can help me move down there, and we'll get a last hurrah before we all traipse off to college.*

Dan couldn't argue with that, or with any reason to spend more time with Abby. She'd visited him in Pittsburgh once a few months ago, and they'd been talking online more or less every week. But two weeks away from parents and chaperones . . . He didn't want to get ahead of himself, but maybe their relationship could finally flourish, or at least survive, with some much-needed quality time together.

The Great Senior Exodus, Jordan had called it. And now, a day after leaving Jordan's miserable parents behind in Virginia, the trip was finally starting to live up to that name.

"These are incredible," Jordan was saying, flicking through the pictures Abby had taken and then uploaded onto his laptop

for safekeeping. "Dan, you should really check these out."

"I know it's kind of cliché, photographing Americana in black and white, but lately I've been obsessing over Diane Arbus and Ansel Adams. They were the focus of my senior project, and Mr. Blaise really loved it."

Dan leaned forward between the seats to look at the photographs with Jordan. "They're definitely worth the stops," he said. They really were something. Open landscapes and deserted buildings—through Abby's eyes, they were desolate, but also beautiful. "So Blaise finally gave you an A, then?"

"Yup. No more stupid A minuses for me." She beamed. Jordan offered up a high five, which Abby managed without taking her eyes off the road. "He actually grew up in Alabama. He's the one who gave me ideas for sites to photograph."

They had already stopped a few—well, *many*—times to allow Abby to take photos, but Dan didn't mind the extra time on the road. He could ride forever in this car with his friends, even if his turns driving got a little tedious.

"I know it's lame to take us so far out of the way, but you're not in too much of a hurry to get there, are you, Jordan?"

"You've already apologized about a million times. Don't worry about it. I'd say something if it was annoying."

"Yes," she said with a laugh. "I'm sure you would."

If he was honest, Dan wasn't in too much of a hurry to get there, either.

It had been nine months since they'd watched the Brookline asylum burn to the ground. The three of them had barely escaped with their lives, and they'd managed that much only with the help of a boy named Micah, who had died trying to buy them time to escape their pursuers. Micah had had a rough, short life, and he'd grown up in Louisiana—a fact Dan had never told Abby or Jordan. Now, just when it seemed like the ghosts of the past were finally content to leave Dan and his friends alone, the three of them were headed to the most haunted city in America. It felt like they were tempting fate, to say the least.

"You okay back there?" Abby asked, cruising smoothly down Highway 59.

"Yeah, I'm good, Abs," Dan said. He wasn't sure if that was a lie. But before Abby could call him on it, Jordan's phone dinged—or rather, a clip of Beyoncé fired off loud enough to make all three of them jump.

Dan knew what that meant. "You're still talking to Cal?"

"On and off," Jordan said, quickly reading the text message. "The on part is why Mom won't pay for school. Not sure what I'd do without Uncle Steve."

"You could stop talking to Cal," Dan suggested.

"And let my parents *win*? Not likely." He peered around the center console at Dan, his bare feet propped up on the dashboard. Late afternoon sunlight glinted off the shiny new black lip piercing Jordan had insisted on getting in Louisville. "He says physical therapy is a real shit show sometimes, but his life feels like paradise after New Hampshire College. Hey! I just realized that at Uncle Steve's, I'll be able to Skype with him without my mother the drama queen bursting into tears."

Dan shifted again, even antsier now at the mention of New Hampshire College. If he let his mind wander or dwell, he would feel the heat of the flames that had engulfed Brookline and everything in it. He wanted to believe that Brookline's effect on him had ended that day—that the evil had died with Warden Crawford and Professor Reyes—but his last moments at the college had given him cause to doubt.

He'd had another vision. He'd seen Micah's ghost, waving good-bye.

He hadn't had any visions since then, and for that, Dan was grateful. It felt like a signal: it was time to let it all go and move on. Even the files and journals he had saved from the ordeal held no interest anymore.

Well, except for one small thing.

Before the trip, Abby and Jordan had threatened to subject Dan to a search of his things for any junk he might have brought from Brookline. They'd said it like a joke—like, no way Dan would really do that to them, right?

But in the end, they hadn't dumped out his bag, which meant they hadn't found the file he had brought along. The one that had been folded in half at the bottom of the stack they'd rescued from Professor Reyes's things. The one labeled *POSSIBLE FAMILY/CONNECTIONS?*, inside which he'd found a paper-clipped pile of papers, connected by a name that had made his heart shoot into his mouth.

MARCUS DANIEL CRAWFORD.

Nine months ago, that pile of papers had seemed like a gift, the reward at the end of a long, hard search for answers about his mysterious past. A sparse family tree had confirmed what he'd already suspected: Marcus was his father, and he was also the nephew of the warden through the warden's youngest brother, Bill. But a single line had also been drawn from Marcus to someone named Evelyn. Was that his mother? It seemed so incomplete. He'd tried to find any Evelyn Crawford online who seemed like a match, but with no promising results and no maiden name, he hadn't had much else to go on.

There was more in the stack—an old postcard, a map, even a police report detailing a time his father had been arrested for breaking and entering—but maddeningly, nothing that would help him pick out his father from the numerous Marcus Daniel Crawfords he found online, and nothing else about his potential mother.

Still. Even after the pile of papers had come to feel less like a gift than a curse, he'd kept the folder hidden. And when he'd packed his bags for this trip, the thought of Paul and Sandy going through his room and finding the folder had been enough to make him bring it—to keep it in sight.

As if on cue, Dan's phone buzzed, not with Beyoncé but with the more subdued jingle indicating Sandy was texting. He checked the message, smiling down into the faint glow of the screen.

How are the intrepid roadtrippers doing? Please tell me you are eating more than beef jerky and Skittles! Call at the next good stopping place.

Dan texted back to reassure her that they were doing their best to eat actual, normal food.

"How's Sandy?" Jordan asked, craning around to look at him again.

"She's good. Just making sure we aren't stuffing ourselves with junk the whole way to Louisiana," Dan replied. He flicked his eyes up to see Jordan swallowing with some difficulty—the insides of his lips were a guilty shade of Skittles orange.

"It's a road trip. What does she think we're going to do?" Jordan asked. "Boil quinoa on the radiator?"

"That's not a half-bad idea," Abby teased. "We are *not* stopping at McDonald's tonight."

"But—"

"No. I checked to see if there was anything to eat other than fast food on the route. Turns out we can avoid the Montgomery traffic and stop at a cute little family-owned diner off 271."

"Diners have hamburgers," Jordan pointed out sagely. "So really, that doesn't change much."

"Hey, I'm just providing a few more options. What you stuff down your gullet is none of my business," she said.

"And thank God for that," Jordan muttered. "Quinoa is for goats."

"I'm with Abby," Dan said. "I could use a salad, or just, you know, a vegetable of any kind. I'm starting to shrivel up from all the beef jerky."

He heard the satisfied smile in Abby's voice as she sat up straighter in the driver's seat and said, "That's settled then. The place I found is called the Mutton Chop, and the same family has owned it for generations. We can get a little local history for my photography project *and* a decent meal."

"I'm still getting a burger," Jordan muttered. He twisted to face the windshield, sighing as he slid down into his seat and began to text at lightning speed. "Soon I'll be on the all-gumbo, all-jambalaya diet. Gotta get my burgers in while I still can."

Chapter 2

*W*hen the tire popping jolted Dan out of a nap, his first thought was to be grateful he wasn't the one driving.

"What was that!" Jordan had shot up like rocket, too, gripping the edge of the door while the car began to swerve and then slow.

"I think we lost a tire," Abby said with a sigh. She didn't seem frightened in the least, holding the wheel steady while the car corrected and then leveled out. She navigated them carefully off the road, letting the Neon idle in the ditch for a second before turning off the ignition. "And that's why you always pack a spare."

"What the hell are we going to do?" Jordan asked, leaning against the window to try to see which tire had blown.

"Paul taught me how to fix tires when I first learned to drive, but I doubt I could manage it," Dan said. They had cell signal, at least, so Triple-A was a possibility.

"Well, lucky for you boys, *I* practiced right before the trip." Patting the wheel with a smug little hop, Abby opened the door and circled to the trunk.

"There'll be no living with her after this," Jordan warned.

"Just be glad she can do it," Dan said. "It's getting dark."

"That's, um, not what I meant."

"Jordan? Jordan! Where is the spare? I know I checked it before I left New York. . . ." Her shout was muted through the windows, but still sharp and getting sharper.

"*That's* what I meant." Jordan sucked in a huge breath, steeling himself, and then eased out of the car. "So, um, before I explain anything, just promise you won't murder me."

"No deal," Abby said. Dan joined them in the cooling night air, watching them square off with matching crossed-arm poses. "Where's the spare, Jordan?"

"Funny story. Remember how my dad was rushing us out the door and I was like, oh, I totally do not need to bring my tauntaun sleeping bag? And then, in the end, I realized that yes, I absolutely, one hundred percent did need to bring it? I'm moving, Abby. Like, for good. I couldn't just leave my tauntaun sleeping bag behind."

Dan snorted behind his wrist, watching Abby's face pale with fury.

"You took out the spare tire to make room for your stupid *Star Trek* memorabilia?"

"Hey, whoa, whoa. I would *not* do that. Star *Wars* memorabilia, on the other hand . . ."

"Whatever it is!" Abby pinched the bridge of her nose, going to inspect the popped tire. She crouched, muttering to herself. "Great. We'll have to walk into town for a spare, then."

"Is it far?" Dan asked, getting out his phone to check the GPS. "Couldn't we just call a tow company?"

"That's way too expensive," Abby replied. "I'm already going to have to buy a new tire, and it's just a half mile more down the road. We almost made it. It wouldn't have been a big deal at all if smarty-pants over here hadn't packed like a twelve-year-old."

"There's nothing to fight about now," Dan said, putting a hand lightly on Abby's shoulder. "And I can kind of see his side. He *is* moving. If he wants New Orleans to feel like home, then he has to bring the stuff he cares about."

"Thank you, Dan. At least two of us understand the value of a tauntaun sleeping bag."

"Stop saying it."

"What?" Jordan smirked. "Tauntaun sleeping bag?"

"Shut. Up. Every time you say that it just makes me want to punch you more," she said, shaking her head. But she was smiling. "That thing better be really warm at least. Maybe I'll borrow it tonight as payback."

✗✗✗✗✗

Nobody had bothered to replace the burned-out neon lights that had once advertised the Mutton Chop. What few bulbs were left told Dan they were eating at the O CH P. The tiny gravel parking lot was packed with cars—mostly rusting trucks. Smoke poured out from some smokestack in the back, filling the air with the salty tang of a greasy-spoon grill.

A mechanic's shop was attached to the building. Not exactly appetizing for the diner, Dan thought, but pretty darn fortunate for them. Food could wait. Abby led them to the door of the garage, but it was dark inside. A scrap of paper on the window read Mechanic Next Door.

The sounds of clinking glasses, country jukebox music, and laughter reached them from the open diner window. A crooked placard next to the screen door seemed to Dan like a warning: "The Mutton Chop! Where everyone knows your face!"

"Where everyone knows your face? Isn't it *name*?" Jordan asked with a snort. "They couldn't even plagiarize properly."

"Don't be a snob, Jordan." Abby opened the screen door, holding it for the boys while they filed through.

"What are you, Saint Abby, protector of the hillbillies?" The noise coming from inside the diner managed to die out in the exact second Jordan finished his sentence. Two dozen heads turned in unison to stare at them. Dan didn't spy many smiles among the crowd. "Of which there are none in this oh-so-charming establishment," Jordan finished, clearing his throat.

"Please stop talking," Abby whispered, turning to address the man who'd walked over and now stood waiting to greet them. Mercifully, the rest of the diners went back to their business.

"Hi there, sir. We were wondering if you could get us the mechanic? Is he here? We blew a tire and need to buy a spare."

The man looked nice enough. He appeared to be in his early twenties, pudgy, and had a short, unkempt beard. He had a name tag that read *JAKE LEE* and grease stains on his coveralls.

"You're in luck, little lady. I'm the mechanic, and a damn good one at that, even if I am just a hillbilly," he said pointedly, shifting his gaze to Jordan. "So, you need a spare tire, eh? What kinda car y'all driving?"

Abby fell into conversation with him, following as he led them back toward the darkened mechanic's shop. She told him she drove a 2007 Neon, and she assured him she had the tools to do the job, just not the tire itself.

He went around to the back of the garage, and in no time at

all he returned with a tire, placing it on the ground in front of them with a heavy *whump*.

"It's getting late, and I'd feel bad letting y'all go back out there alone. You sure you know what you're doing?" He took off his baseball cap and ruffled his sparse hair. He looked directly at Abby, watching her struggle to roll the new tire onto its side.

"Could you give us a ride back to the car? I'd really appreciate it. We were planning to stop in the diner for dinner, but it'd be better if we could bring our car back here before it gets too dark."

Jake Lee nodded, then turned and marched off in the direction of his enormous pick-up. "Might be a tight squeeze. Truck's meant for haulin' stuff, not people."

"That's fine," Abby said. "Thanks for helping us out." Dan had no idea how she could keep up such a bright demeanor while she tried to maneuver the tire into the flatbed of the truck. Dan dashed over to help, and then Jordan joined, too.

"No trouble at all," Jake said.

Dan hoped this was just friendly Southern hospitality at work. He couldn't help feeling a creepy vibe from this guy and his willingness to help them. But it was already getting dark, and if they had to walk back to the car with that heavy tire it would take them way too long.

They piled into the front cab of the truck, Jordan whimpering from the sudden onslaught of about sixteen car fresheners stuffed behind the rearview mirror. "Maybe I'd rather walk," he whispered. "What smell do you think he's trying to cover up?"

"I'd rather not think about it," Dan whispered back.

Jake Lee drove them back up the road, humming softly as they went. When that started to get weird, he turned on the radio, and

bluegrass blasted out of the tinny speakers, so loud and frantic it immediately gave Dan a headache.

Abby remained all smiles, hopping out of the truck when they reached the Neon. Without prompting, Jake Lee parked and lowered the gate on the truck bed, grunting and sweating as he pulled the spare onto the gravel ditch.

"Here now," he said, lumbering back to the cab and getting an enormous flashlight. "Take this. You can give it back to me when you get in to the diner for supper."

"That's really nice of you," Abby said, fetching the little tool kit and jack from the back of the car. Dan heard her sigh at the sight of the sleeping bag rolled up where the spare tire ought to be. He took up the position of spotlight operator, holding the big yellow bulb steady while Abby set to work.

He glanced at Jake Lee, who had paused on the way back to his truck to watch them. More than watch them, really—he was staring, his head cocked to the side like he'd just discovered a rare species of insect and was trying to decide what to do with it. Dan tried to give a friendly wave to get his attention, but the mechanic just frowned and shook his head before driving off into the night.

The images in this book are custom photo illustrations
created by Faceout Studio and feature photographs from actual asylums,
real vintage carnivals, and found photographs from New Orleans.

PAGE	TITLE	FROM THE COLLECTION OF
i, iii	Girl	Anna Mutwil / Arcangel Images
	Gate	Roy Bishop / Arcangel Images
	Texture	Naoki Okamoto / Getty Images
	Photo borders	iStockphoto

THE SCARLETS

PAGE	TITLE	FROM THE COLLECTION OF
vii	Skull	croisy / Thinkstock
28	Dark bedroom	mile84 / Thinkstock
31	Writing on wall	mdulieu / Thinkstock
38	Child	Susan Stevenson / Thinkstock
		Ultrashock / Shutterstock
43	University hallway	genemcc / Thinkstock
66	Goth girl	kobrin_photo / Thinkstock
75	Cloaked figure running	Jupiterimages / Thinkstock
86	Creepy, damaged room	Fotokon / Shutterstock
89	Cloaked figure with stake	Nazina_Maryna / Thinkstock
		Uros Petrovic / Thinkstock
	Chapter openers	*pp. x, 2, 7, 17, 24, 34, 39, 45, 52, 58, 62, 67, 72, 80*
	Paper texture	Eky Studio / Shutterstock
	Diamond background	Carol Abram / Shutterstock

THE BONE ARTISTS

THE WARDEN

202	Wrought iron gate	Jacques PALUT / Shutterstock
208	Creepy hallway	wang song / Shutterstock
215	Hanging lightbulb	Nikolay Popov / Thinkstock
227	Porcelain head	Mark Frost / Thinkstock
247	Warden Crawford's door	Wally Gobetz / Library of Congress nuttakit / Shutterstock
266	Nurse in white mask	Olaru Radian alexandru / Thinkstock
277	Heels on stairs	Michel Stevelmans / Shutterstock Photosani / Thinkstock
280	Hammer	t81 / Shutterstock Steve Collender / Shutterstock
Chapter openers		*pp. 196, 198, 203, 218, 223, 241, 251, 257, 273* Alex Roman

ASYLUM

PAGE	TITLE	FROM THE COLLECTION OF
287	Girl in doorway Texture	Carmen Gonzalez / Trevillion Images Naoki Okamoto / Getty Images
293	Brookline	James W. Rosenthal, Library of Congress
Chapter openers		*pp. 288, 290, 295* Alex Roman

SANCTUM

PAGE	TITLE	FROM THE COLLECTION OF
299	Girl in hallway Texture	Eva van Oosten / Trevillion Images Naoki Okamoto / Getty Images

CATACOMB